A TIME TRAVEL THRILLER

THE RECKONING

D.M. TAYLOR

ISBN: 978-1-7345442-0-6 (E BOOK)
ISBN: 978-1-7345442-1-3 (PAPERBACK)

Cover Design by 100Covers.com
Interior Design by FormattedBooks.com

Quantum
Entanglement
Publishing

For my mom who seeded the desire within to time travel

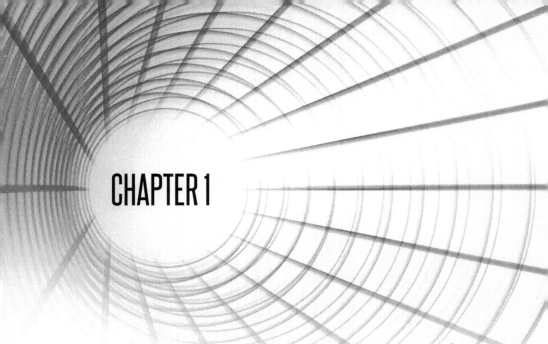

CHAPTER 1

flashbulb memory-n. A vivid and detailed memory of the moment significant news was received.

The snow covered building, lined with too many windows to count, housed the laboratories which birthed my visions of time. The parking lot was fairly empty due to the off hours I kept.

I walked through the main doors where Maxine, our weekend guard, greeted me. She waved me through security from her high top chair, calling me 'sweet girl' as she did every day. Past her prime, Maxine had clear ideas about what a woman should be doing with her life. She always told me, "It's the weekend honey! You should let that handsome man of yours take you out on the town rather than work every minute of your life."

But, Maxine didn't understand how my pace quickened heading towards my offices, how my pulse jolted with each step. Swiping my badge to grant my entrance made me more aware I was alive. Pushing the glass doors open welcomed contentment to wash over me. I could never explain why I could be so fully in charge and self assured here but then come undone in every other part of my life. The same sterile white background was in my kitchen at home, but here it never felt like a splash of color was needed to improve upon the place. The color here could be found in the work and the people doing it.

Not completely unusual, everyone was in flux. This hubbub throughout the room seemed to be a result of the internet and phone outage. I had assumed it was only a problem with my service provider, but it appeared to be happening here as well.

My crew looked as if an apocalypse had begun. Dakotah rushed forward as I made my way within.

"Taden, what is happening? Have you heard anything?"

Assuming she referred to the Internet and phones not working I responded with acute surprise to find that communications at the lab could be out as well.

 Earlier, I stared at the screen of my computer, hair in wet braids after my shower, drinking coffee in the small apartment claimed as a place to pass my time when not working. I had actually just finished reading my mail online (physical mail being, as of last year, a thing of the past). Then, filled myself spiritually, hunting for meaningful words to save, meditate on, and revisit later to remind myself about what's important, who is important, and the fact that I would never let go of my mom.

Sometimes, it didn't feel like I had the right to keep holding on to her since she had been gone for so long, but there had to be people who still loved and ached for those they lost long ago. I stumbled across a profound quote by Candace Lightner, "Grief comes in three stages. The beginning. The middle. The rest of your life." I read it over several times, making it my mantra for the day.

I dragged myself back into the kitchen littered with remnants of last night's dinner for another cup of coffee, promising myself to definitely clean up the mess after this last cup. I was wishing Marius was here instead of at work. He always did the dishes after dinner and I didn't feel quite so lonely in this apartment with him here.

With my laptop in hand, I settled back onto my oversized couch in front of the bay window and pulled a blanket over myself noticing it smelled of his cologne. Looking out the window at the winter world outside, I wondered if any interesting conversations were happening online. I feel slightly less incompetent when conversations are done through keystrokes versus my actual mouth—which does not edit as well.

A heated debate among a few of my friends about the desperate state of our country was in progress.

Our last elected president had served his full, politically corrupt term in office. It was a marked period of division among citizens in the country, as well as a frightening repeat of historical events we failed to learn from. When it came time to finally elect a new president, our democratic process had become so hijacked that for the first time since presidential elections began, a successor was chosen by the sitting President himself, to the shock and dismay of many citizens. Although the President's son had taken over without the consent of the people, nothing impeded the beginning of this appalling dynasty. Instead of demanding we return to democratic process, our society had become distracted by a parade of blaming and unrest.

Even though it was mind numbing to read the comments people left online, still my participation felt obligatory. An ongoing debate had singled out one political party as the reason to fault our failed democracy. My natural curiosity led me to wonder if the people writing these words actually believed them. Was it their truth, or merely a coping mechanism for living in a country that had effectively stripped us of our democratic rights? However bleak it felt, in the midst of all of this turmoil I *knew* we still had hope as a country. My work with the government was intended in some way to fix the weakened structure.

However bleak, it felt necessary to participate in these types of discussions to challenge thought processes and negate the senseless propaganda. In the midst of typing my questions for the group, my connection went.

Not thinking anything of it at first, I closed it out and logged back in but couldn't reconnect. A quick check revealed my phone's internet wasn't working either. Like my sister always suggested, I tried turning it off and back on again to see if it would do the trick but it didn't. My initial reaction was frustration.

In a huff, I walked back to the kitchen to make myself a sandwich, consciously placing my food on a paper plate so as to not deposit more dishes into my already full sink. While standing at the counter in my desolate, disheveled kitchen eating my sandwich, I listened to the monthly test alarm ringing outside.

Old dependable. As far back as memory served, the first Saturday of the month right at 1 p.m. the alarm would ring. It was almost peaceful to hear the obnoxious alarm. A sense of security came from this regular practice alarm. It made me feel as if a true catastrophe were to happen, we would be safe.

Out my kitchen window, the view of Gaithersberg, Maryland was a gray-slush lifeless day. After the test alarm, I called my sister to see what she was up to on this *beautiful* Saturday afternoon. Her window would be displaying a dreamlike, sunshiny, palm tree stay-cation. Weather was not really a topic I ever enjoyed, but I *did* want to hear her voice and see how her day was going.

The phone call wouldn't go through. At this point, a pang of concern triggered in my conscious thought.

Insignificant nagging in the back of my mind transformed to the precise moment of accepting the knowledge that something was *wrong*. My thoughts scrambled through unacknowledged evidence. *The internet isn't working, phone calls won't go through.* And then my thoughts danced around the idea that the usual Saturday test alarm might have possibly been more than a test.

It's hard to describe how it felt to become abruptly cut off. Normally, every second of every day I could know what everyone was doing, where they were, how they felt, and what their political stance was. I could read my mail, do my banking, my shopping, and fill myself spiritually all in the device held in my hand.

Then, I couldn't.

It felt empty.

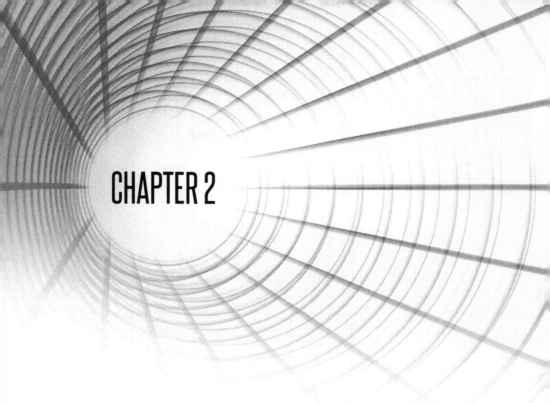

CHAPTER 2

Exasperated and unblinking, her eyes widened. Dakotah held up three forefingers and blurted, "The three key Patriot Party leaders are waiting for you in your office. Apparently a great national security has been breached with initial stages of attack on the Federal Communications Commission. No one in the entire country can make phone calls, go online, get television or even radio reception."

Dakotah took a deep breath before she continued the rest of her update. Like a conductor of an orchestra setting up for a massive crescendo, she raised her left hand towards me, palm flat as if to tell me to stop talking, which I wasn't even thinking about doing. I absolutely had no words at this point.

"And Taden, if you think that's hard to believe, you are *not* going to believe this next part. They are here to brief *you* about it." She nudged me along the corridor to my office in a hurry.

Her string of words were hard to believe. I had never been privy to national security before. The fact that I'd been acquired by the government to discover a technology *they* wanted had never before meant being a part of any security briefings. Of course, my natural curiosity would lead me to question my bosses and come to my own conclusions regarding the purpose of my discoveries. The main objective to this mission seemed quite obvious with the dismantling of our democracy taking place. The details of how and why were not a part of this scientist's agenda, though.

In an anxiety-induced hysteria, I turned to Dakotah, desperately hoping she might know more. All she could do at this point was escort me to the room where *it* was about to happen. Whatever *it* was.

My nerves were wrapped around themselves, tightening across all parts of my body responsible for breathing as I kept walking. Upon reaching the windows outside my office, Dakotah stopped to watch the rest out of eyesight, which meant I was on my own. A quick count confirmed there were indeed three quite serious agents in intimidating dark uniforms with equally dark expressions hanging on their faces.

The woman, with deep raven hair, black eyes, and a jawline so sharp it could cut open a box, was Danica Farkas, head director of the Patriot Party. Along with her was Joseph Warren, who reminded me of my Dad: Tall, thin, looking like he must be somewhere very important very soon. The third person was Bernard Richardson. He was clearly the muscle in the room—he stood strongly on guard, ready to save us all if needed.

They were waiting for me in stone silence. Blushing with embarrassment, I considered they could have been waiting a while…a minor detail I forgot to find out from Dakotah. Simultaneously, I noticed the piles of paper spread across my desk and the many messy stacks of them scattered at random throughout my office.

For a woman of science at my level it was just as embarrassing that I still used paper notebooks as it was to have such a disheveled office.

Without missing a beat, my face pulled into an important businesslike expression before entering through the office door, pausing once at the awareness that it felt as if *I* was the guest here.

"Welcome," I said as I made eye contact with each of the agents. "Ms. Farkas, Mr. Richardson, Mr. Warren. I apologize for keeping you waiting. It has been a strange morning and I wasn't able to call the office. I had no idea you were coming today, or I certainly would have been better prepared for your visit. How can I help my fellow Patriots?"

Bernard, still standing closest to me near the glass door, closed it with his foot. Once the door was shut, Danika, sitting at *my* desk, gestured for me to take a seat in the chair next to Joseph, who had been watching me with a masked expression. Danika's powerful presence at my modest laminate desk was an oxymoron. A throne would've better suited her. She spoke with a hint of desperation as I sat down, full of anticipation, on one of the chairs across from her.

"Dr. Barrett, we are here this afternoon to find out how close you are to your breakthrough."

Obvious from the grim tone in the room, this impromptu meeting with the Patriot Party wasn't simply an update on my work. Normally, these meetings were scheduled well in advance with an agenda to follow, a process I much preferred to this surprise visit.

Clearing my throat, I said, "I'm actually glad that you're here today. We *are* on the verge of being able to test time travel on humans. My team has cracked the process of leaping backwards into the time continuum, though only in increments of minutes, so far. I can take you to the lab and show you a demonstration if—"

Danika inched forward in my chair and widened her eyes with purpose as she interrupted my offer. "You have it then? We need this to be a priority."

A priority? This is my entire life. It is the ONLY priority I have ever had.

The devastation of my mom's death split my universe into two time periods: before she died and after.

Feeling special, before mom died. First knowing I would be a scientist, before mom died. Meeting my mentor, Dr. Pasterski, before mom died. Starting high school, before mom died. Being an orphan, after mom died. Spending all my free time assisting Dr. Pasterski, after mom died. Getting a full scholarship to UPenn, after mom died. Landing the most amazing job of my life, after mom died. *The Reckoning*, after Mom died.

No.

Wait.

That was before Mom died.

The time Dad spent with me, we were always building or fixing things around the house. He was generally busy with work so when he was with me, our time was consumed with putting together or taking things apart.

The love of science was given to me from both of my parents, not just my dad. Another reason my life went down this path was a result of my mom, Elizabeth Barrett, who was my biggest supporter.

Because my parents believed in me with such conviction, I had to buy into some of their faith—even just a fraction. As a result, my self-proclamation of being a scientist was built on solid ground from which I did not waver.

For three years after her cancer diagnosis, my sister Ruth and I watched our fiercely independent, perceptively gorgeous mother become solely dependent on us to do basic, everyday things. We already had to suffer one parent's death. It wasn't fair.

People were drawn to her features, then got hooked on her personality, and finally were left longing to be near her when she was gone. She was a woman who gave herself to others in countless selfless ways. *This is what my mom got in return?* If only her dying could've gone quicker. The pain of losing her suddenly would've been relentless, but her death wasn't about us. Instead, she put up a long, drawn out fight, so that by the time my weakened mother lost her battle, she had also lost her dignity, her beauty had betrayed her, and the giving nature she blessed people with was hollowed from unspeakable pain, day in and day out.

To be Elizabeth's daughter meant the horror of knowing I could not take her pain away. On top of all she had endured, in her slow loss Elizabeth's teenage daughter actually had the nerve to be angry with her. I avoided spending any time with her at the end.

I was angry that she wasn't fighting hard enough to be here with me. I was angry that she needed me so much. I was angry that she still thought she could be my mom instead of the other way around.

Years after my mom's death, shame took residence in my soul for my final treatment of her. When she passed away, I was honestly shocked. The rest of the world knew it would be any day. We had hospice care visiting every day while we two girls went to school.

My mom's nurse did her best to prepare Ruth and me to say goodbye, but I was still trapped in the mindset that she was going to win this fight.

The night she died, my mom wasn't feeling well. I mean, worse than normal. She had picked up a sinus infection or a head cold earlier that week and was miserable. Despite her added misery, still, I went to Dr. Pasterski's house next door to help with an investigation she was running. Ruth, being the older sister, the one who was now caring for my well being as well as our mother's, said for me to go.

"But be back for bedtime. I don't want to have to walk next door to remind you, and Dr. Pasterski has way more important things to do than tell you to go home."

"Understood!" I knew full well she could use a break, but I got on my bike anyway. I paused at our apartment building long enough for the thought to register—*I really should stay here with her*—but kept on peddling to the part of my world that made sense: science.

Later, on my way back home, Ruth's screaming could be heard from the street. By the time I reached inside our home, she was splayed across our mom. Her long brown hair tangled down her back and matted across her tear-soaked face. Her arms wrapped around Mom, squeezing with ferocity, begging her not to die. This image of Ruth is forever seared into my brain. She looked so tiny and fragile on top of our cancer-beaten mother.

I was too late. My mom passed on without me. Maybe it was for the best, not having to watch my mom leave. Maybe the choice to keep pedaling rather than come home was what haunted me. Deep down, perhaps I knew this was my last goodbye, but ignored my gut.

I stood frozen inside the doorway, staring at Ruth trying to physically pull our mom back to us. Without conscious thought, the key gripped so tightly in my fist was thrown from my hands as if they were on fire. My feet couldn't move fast enough as I stumbled backward out of our apartment to escape the nightmare playing out before my eyes.

My mind was a jumble, my sight blurred to the brink of blindness. My whereabouts were familiar but conscious decisions were not in my mental capacity. Persistent screams broke from my soul into the crisp evening air, stopping only to allow sobbing to take hold of me and throw my body onto the cold, hard concrete.

Dr. Pasterski discovered me. She had a friend with her whom I found myself absently wondering about before remembering my fresh orphan status. They must have heard me from inside and came out to find where the screams were coming from. Ruth joined us minutes after. She was still crying and her face was swelling to the point that it looked like it belonged to someone else. Once the two women learned the news of my mom's death from my sister, they each took hold of an arm and half carried, half walked me back home. Poor Ruth trailed behind us, shuddering with tiny whimpers. Dr. Pasterski seemed out of sorts and her appearance wasn't as smooth and put together as it usually was.

Back inside our home, Dr. Pasterski said goodbye to her friend but stayed with me and Ruth the rest of the night, helping us deal with hospice and all the other adult responsibilities we needed to attend to. Ruth was already busy cleaning up bed linens and medical things. In disbelief, I sat on the couch, my head buried in Dr. Pasterski's arms. It was safe to say, this was the worst night of my life.

But of course Danika was talking about the priorities of the Patriot Party, not mine.

I looked her in the eyes with the very level of confidence my reputation had earned me and responded with assurance, "I understand. Most recently we have been working on single-cell organisms with success, and we are now in the initial stages of testing more complex life forms in longer timeframes. It is clear to me at this point, though, that we are not able to send into the future. We can only go backward into the past as far as the living organism's lifespan, and from that distance in time return to the present."

Danika again interrupted me. "Dr. Barrett, you must know some of what has happened today?" Shaking my head slowly with surprise, I knew she couldn't be referring to the communication issue.

Besides my basic knowledge that this technology was meant to save our democracy, I felt the major push for my country was to be the first to discover time travel. Since day one of my career at the NIST, although I felt the desire to have this technology as soon as possible, I had not felt the sense of urgency that Danika now implied.

Danika spoke, "I will be brief, so as to let you get back to the vital job you serve for our country. Today, at 1 p.m., several states were taken over by a team of radicals who call themselves The Reckoning. They are working together with the goal of breaking apart the United States and recolonizing the territory claimed. What we know so far is that all of the internet towers, cable, radio, and phone lines have been intercepted and jammed to no longer function. The Reckoning has taken advantage of our alarm testing systems by attacking at a time when people would assume the sirens as routine testing. Now all of our communications are jammed including the alarm systems. Our country is at war and no one knows. Maryland is an important key location that we need to keep from being taken. We have decided to shift the purpose of our time travel mission away from the presidential debacle onto this more immediate crisis. The ability to travel back will allow us to target the exact location in time that The Reckoning was initiated and put an end to it before it even begins. Our intelligence has been investigating exactly what is happening and who The Reckoners are for many years. This has allowed us to begin tracing it backwards. Most recently, you have been working on the piece that will get us there. Now, you must be perfecting your technology so that we can all be ready for action as soon as possible."

She told me all of this matter-of-factly, barely batting an eyelash, while I held my mouth gaped open. My ears were ringing and I couldn't quite grasp she had told me our country was under attack and I was supposed to take a part in *saving* it. The scenario Danika had laid out for me sounded like a fictional story—but then I *was* working on time travel. Trying to gather myself and look like the professional, respected scientist who had devoted her life to the study, I closed my mouth and swallowed hard.

Collecting my wits, I said, "You will be updated regularly with any other breakthroughs made."

At first, I ignored it like a nagging sensation, but her name got louder and louder until I unintentionally blurted, "Ruth."

The two other agents walked out of my office; only Danika turned in response. "I'm sorry, what was that, Dr. Barrett?"

"Oh," I responded breathlessly pausing in dismay after hearing her name out loud. "Ruth! My sister! She lives in California. Is L.A. safe? Has it been attacked?" My voice lifted a little higher every sentence until I barely finished the last word.

She studied my face for a moment, like maybe she was considering if I could handle her answer. Then, decidedly, she responded, "I apologize Dr. Barrett. California was one of the first states to be taken. We are working to amend this issue. It is the plan to save your sister and everyone else involved. Remember: your role is imperative. Please focus your energy into your work." Respectfully nodding her head, she turned to follow Bernard who was waiting for her outside the door.

And just like that, I was alone.

CHAPTER 3

Ruth, my sister, was eighteen when my mom died. It became her job to raise me. While she did make sure I stayed focused the rest of high school, cooked me dinner, and kept the laundry going, truly we raised each other from then on. She needed me as much as I needed her, especially considering she had become addicted to opiates she stole from my mom the night she died.

Most nights, I would do homework while Ruth sat on Mom's favorite blue couch, staring out the window. She'd look vacant, and I would wonder where she had gone in her thoughts, worried if I wasn't there to bring her back she would have gotten lost.

I harbored guilt for how much first-hand death experience Ruth had to live through while I ran off to consume my mind with physics. I wish I would have been more present during the dark time so she didn't have to suffer through it alone. Maybe she wouldn't have taken the drugs if I had been around more.

It took me much too long to realize that Ruth was using my mom's morphine and oxycodone to numb her pain. How many evenings did she pop a pill and drift away from the loneliness while I was gone? Her irritability with me grew day by day. I felt like it was deserved so I didn't question it, but my suspicion piqued at the clearer signs of warning; she stayed in her room all the time, she was not concerned at all with eating, and our home was looking more like a frat house by the day.

I didn't really care about the mess, but it was totally out of character for my sister. My entire life, Ruth had been quite careful about her living conditions. At first, it was excusable to pass it off as grief, but it went beyond that and I was starting to worry about her. I walked in on her one night sedated across her bed. She wasn't asleep, but certainly not coherent enough to talk to me. The TV was playing some stupid show she always used to watch with our mom. I had never seen a person strung out on drugs before but I felt certain that's what I was looking at with my sister.

The secret was buried for fear that if anyone found out, Ruth would be deemed unfit to care for me and I would become custody of the state. My routines changed the next day with visits to Dr. Pasterski's cut down to only a few days a week. The drugs were almost gone by the time I caught on to their presence, which led to a natural intervention process of quitting them slowly and providing her the emotional support she needed when there were no more left to dull her feelings. I didn't judge her. My drug of choice was science. There was no end to that. I truly felt bad she lost her escape, even though we both knew it would kill her.

There was one certainty about her: Ruth was in the wrong part of the world. She was not created for snow to blanket around her, and most definitely not meant for the regular falling of water from the Maryland sky. She was a daughter of the sun and needed to be wrapped in the warmth of that bright star. Ruth only stuck around to take care of me. My guilt didn't lessen any knowing I was still causing her pain.

"How's your homework going, Taden?" she would ask, like she could feel me studying her across the room.

I'd scan her petite facial features for signs of distress, or notice how many times she would flip her hazelnut hair from side to side while she sat there. These were indicators that Ruth needed a break from the adult life she was thrust into.

"I'm gettin' it done. How about you? Your math getting solved out our window?" I gave her a sassy grin because I knew she had caught me watching her.

"Actually, I happen to do my best thinking looking out this window."

What I know now is that she was thinking about me, and if I was going to be alright. This was our relationship, two orphans taking care of each other.

It was difficult to leave her when I was accepted to the University of Pennsylvania. Several scholarships that would ultimately guide my choice to attend school there. I considered not going, but she wouldn't hear it, reminding me, "This is what Mom and Dad would've wanted for you, Taden. It was always the plan. You have to do this for them."

It wasn't until Ruth told me her plan to leave Maryland that I finally agreed to go away to school. This was the opportunity she needed to start fresh, to leave Maryland with its long cold winters behind to go where she had always dreamed of being a beach girl. As far as she was concerned, only California could deliver her much-needed Vitamin D.

Ruth and I went our separate ways after mom died. It was the last personal connection I had for many years. While we did video call each other every single day, we only saw each other in person a few times a year. After I began my job at the NIST, it started to become normal (and contractually obligatory) to withhold some life details from her. I'd settled comfortably into being a lonely island.

My work became my whole life. Of course, I acquired working relationships with my peers. They respected me for my focus and drive. However, I was acutely aware that the very aspect that drove respect also prevented true understanding. Beyond my research, there was not much to me, unless you were my sister. I talked to my sister every day. What I wouldn't give to talk to my parents again.

My life's focus drove me to devote every ounce of brainpower in my ability to beat the clock. To go back. To be there for my sister. To see my mom again. The night she died, I couldn't live with it. Regret was the core of who I had become in this world.

I was with Dr. Pasterski when we first decided to tackle time travel—wait, was it then, or later? I could remember time travel with my mom alive. To me, it was a fascinating concept. I delivered our ideas and theories to my mom with reverence. When it finally happened, she was there, but she was sick. Maybe The Reckoning was before Mom died but so close I couldn't quite discern if it was before or after. *Which would mean I was in high school when I discovered time travel?* That can't be right. *When did this happen?*

Whenever it happened, it was with Dr. Pasterski, the Einstein of her age, my neighbor and mentor. I followed up on the science all through college, and submitted my proposal for my thesis on time travel—but UPenn refused my proposal. While wallowing in self pity, I was stunned to be propositioned by the government. My thesis theories had been passed up by my university on direct orders of The Patriot Party.

Dr. Pasterski, it turned out was a major player in the agency and had been grooming me for this since I was a young girl. The Patriots explained they had been watching my performance with serious considerations at her urging since high school. My scholarship to The University of Pennsylvania had been completely funded by them. It was anyone's guess who funded this agency, since it was not even on the radar of any federal agencies within the United States including and especially the president and his cabinet.

My mission was clear: I would work at the National Institute of Science and Technology as a physicist, my objective to execute the theories in my thesis to develop time travel for the Patriots—and for myself.

While my mission was always clear to me, I could never tell my sister. In fact, the only people besides myself who could know my mission were my teammates—who, thankfully, I was able to assemble myself. It took almost a year to find the right candidates. They had to be people I trusted and could be in charge of, to help me execute my ideas.

Marius Touma was my first selection. He entered the room with an air of confidence and a smile which seemed individually crafted for me. Not a hint of nervous energy could be detected during his interview. At points, I felt he was interviewing me.

"It is a pleasure to finally meet you, Dr. Barrett. I've read all your published works. The piece you did at UPenn on the initiation of their physics and astronomy club for women was particularly intriguing. I feel honored that you would consider working with me."

My cheeks became warm, and I realized I was blushing in response to him. I hadn't expected my first candidate to be making this interview about me. Avoiding his eyes while I regained my composure, I responded, "I'm impressed, Mr. Touma. You've done your research."

"Please, call me Marius. Mr. Touma makes me sound like my dad."

His movements were slow and deliberate and his words controlled and open ended. He looked around the lab as we walked through toward my office.

"What kind of magic happens here?"

My smile at his question felt childish. Instead of giving him an answer to a question about my work, I gave him a schoolgirl grin. He was comfortable with proximity, which is why I noticed he smelled like a mix of rosemary, clove, and young love. It was exciting to be around his electric energy, yet I dreaded the prospect of sitting in my office alone with Marius. How many more times would I blush in his presence? He sat in the chair across from my desk and instinctively pulled it closer toward me. My eyes widened at his boldness but he didn't seem to notice. Instead, he continued to look into them as he spoke.

"What would you like to know about me?"

Then, he waited patiently for my response, in no rush to force his story upon me. As I honed into my own questions, he shared freely any history I asked of him. His list of accomplishments were a mile long. I asked him what motivated his career moves.

"That's a heavy question Dr. Barrett. Am I able to call you Taden, moving forward?" It seemed like a wonderful prospect to have him want to do so. Again, I blushed. Again, I smiled, while nodding. "Good. Alright then, Taden, what motivates me in my career and personal life is to make my little sister proud. She always looked up to me and saw me as a hero. She died when we were kids." He looked down for the first time since his interview began.

"Oh, I'm so sorry. I didn't know. It's very sweet." He looked back up at me. "My mom died when I was fifteen. I get what you're saying."

This time, he smiled at me and my heart skipped a few beats. "Thank you for sharing that with me, Taden."

A major difference between Marius and I was that he had a charming nature and loved to be immersed into a crowd. It actually made me consider not choosing him for the team. However, I came to my senses, realizing the discriminatory nature of not hiring a perfect candidate just because I found him interesting to look at and somewhat charming. I simply had to hold myself to a higher accountability when I was around him, and for God's sake stop blushing so much.

Dakotah Hughs was my next selection. When I came across her file, the projects she had been a part of had intrigued me first. Dakotah's clearest strength was the research she had done in her field of biophysics, with well-founded breakthroughs in radiation certain to be beneficial for our team.

In our first meeting, what struck me most was how comfortable I was with the idea of trusting her. She had striking green eyes, something I noticed not only because of how compelling they were but because she had no problem holding eye contact with me when she spoke. This level of confidence gave me the impression that she wasn't hiding anything about herself.

Over time, I learned that her mornings were spent carefully focused on resetting her thoughts through meditation, opening her body with yoga, manifesting abundance by practicing gratefulness & goal setting, then finally self love via killer outfits that made her feel awesome. It was a shame her clothes were always covered up by a white lab coat. As a result, by the time she got to her hair there was no more time, so up in a ponytail it went. Dakotah spoke truths without a fleck of hesitation for how she would be perceived.

In just one interview I was clear about who Dakotah was and what she stood for. If I was looking for a team to help finalize the search for time travel, I needed to believe in them, and I believed in Dakotah's brains, her boldness, and her beautiful eyes from the start.

The last (but not least) pick for our team was Abel Mihal, who came recommended by Dr. Pasterski herself. He too graduated from Penn in the physics department and I knew him from different projects we had collaborated on over the years we both spent working on our undergrad and grad studies there. His intelligence and logic had always been impressive. Abel was not show-boaty like Marius, and he didn't have strength in his presence like Dakotah, but he was devoted.

It was from working alongside him that my admiration grew. It was also from working alongside him that I noticed he was nicely built (extremely disciplined about working out every day when he woke up) and had the longest eyelashes I had ever seen on a man. Like me, he wasn't very comfortable with eye contact but was more of an observer. I've felt him looking at me many times with his soft brown eyes. Abel really understood other people and was a spot-on judge of character. You could never question Abel's devotion to anything or anyone. If he chose to do something, or to talk to someone, he was fully committed. He was not one to split his attention between tasks and people.

In all, there were four of us. My team of three included Dakotah, Abel, and Marius; a team of coverts. We couldn't breathe a word of our life inside the lab to anyone. We only had each other…and time travel.

Marius, Dakotah, and Abel. After mom died. I'm pretty sure.

 Minutes had passed behind the Patriot Party leaving my office, but still I hung onto Danika's words: "save your sister." Still not having made a single movement, the tingling, light-headed feeling slowly alerted me to the fact that I was holding my breath.

Just as I was purposefully re-engaging with the breathing process, Marius came bursting through my office doors, his eyes locked on me. He swiveled me around with his hands on my shoulders and waited. I looked into his eyes, then quickly shifted my gaze down.

When he could stand it no more, Marius implored, "Taden, what did they say?"

I looked back up at him. He seemed concerned but not shaken. He *almost* looked excited. It was well known that Marius thrived on moments in which his adrenaline could kick in. The Patriots' visit was enough to nearly overdose him.

Typically, it is a quality I find magnetic about him. His energy can ignite my own to a higher level. In the wake of all I had just learned I didn't feel seduced to match Marius's surge. He didn't notice my lack of engagement even though it was highly unusual for me not to become captivated with his exuberance.

"It's Ruth, she's in trouble." He deflated.

"Is she okay?" he asked. "Why would the Patriots be here to tell you something about Ruth?"

"I need to start from the beginning. All communications have been compromised, throughout the country. Several states have been taken over by a radical group called The Reckoning with the apparent goal of breaking apart the United States. California was one of the first to be taken. Ruth is in California. That's all I know right now. I am supposed to be focused on completing my job so the government can use our time travel to undo this catastrophe."

His soul seemed to soar again. The ignition he needed to jumpstart his drive. Although I wished he was more appalled by my news, I loved him. I loved being the recipient of his attention so when he placed one of his hands on my face and gently kissed my cheek saying "Let's go save your sister," I followed his lead.

As we walked out of the office I saw Abel standing in the doorway, watching the end of our exchange. From his facial expressions, I could see how deeply concerned he was. He opened his mouth to say something and then changed his mind. Forcing a half smile as we approached his direction, he returned a sympathetic smile back to me.

At the last minute, Abel decided to say what he was holding back, "Foot soldiers just informed us California has been taken over by terrorists. Parts of New York have also been infiltrated." And with that, he quickly walked off ahead of us toward the lab.

News that New York had been infiltrated in any way shocked me. We followed Abel back and my thoughts ping ponged between Ruth and The Reckoning. *New York?* It was so close, and such a strong representation of America. *This was really happening?!*

Like a starting line in the race for my sister's life, as soon as I crossed through the threshold back into the lab, I began my task to save Ruth and my country. In that order.

"Our mission has changed. We need to accelerate our work." Marius looked at me out of the corner of his eye, already busy setting up the measurements.

Dakotah had been back at her computer since the Patriots left. She stopped for the first time to acknowledge my announcement and nodded her head with respect.

Abel was standing next to me, waiting for me to continue but staring at Marius. *Was he waiting for orders?* I didn't mean to come off as their sergeant but now that this had become a national priority involving my only living family member it had to have a new level of dedication from me. I was in charge and needed to step into my role like never before.

"Abel, why don't you help Marius get the vials set up for the serum mixtures and calibrate the gauges to begin reading today's magnitudes."

He nodded his head in agreement and began to silently adjust the apparatus that Marius would need to complete his work.

Marius sighed a slight breath of irritation and rolled his eyes. It wasn't clear who his response was for, me or Abel—but I didn't have time to invest another second thinking about it.

All I could manage to hold onto in my brain was the fact that Ruth could be in danger.

It was already a year ago that we celebrated our first substantial breakthrough. At that point our team had been working together for over a year before Marius and I ended up pulling an overnight shift. It was the first time our team had successfully sent something back in time. Symbolically, we had chosen a pocket watch as our test sample. We needed to monitor and collect data every hour for a full forty-eight hours while the watch was theoretically sitting in the past, so of course, I stayed.

Moderately shocking, with quick fervor, Marius volunteered to stay with me that night. I expected to be pulling this gig alone. Dakotah and Abel seemed as surprised as me. In response, they both offered to stay as well, but it seemed obvious they were only offering because Marius did.

He refuted their offers. "No need, the two of us are enough. You guys go home and get a good night's sleep. You'll both need to be fresh to replace us in the morning when we're ready to crash." Dakotah and Abel could have won an Oscar, acting the part of reluctantly resigning, before they went home to rest. No one wanted to miss anything major, but sleep was highly valued among this crowd.

The first couple of hours were normal business with Marius. We monitored data every hour. We chatted over usual small talk. He offered to run out and get us dinner. Before I could even respond, he had put on his coat and was out the door. It was weird that he didn't ask me what I wanted or where he should go but I had other, more important tasks requiring my attention.

After a short time, he was back with my favorite take out from the Lebanese bistro a few blocks away, a bottle of wine, and two paper cups. This was both interesting and unnerving to me.

"I got your favorite," he announced while unpacking the bags that held our dinner.

"I see, thank you. You didn't have to do that," I said, my voice reaching a higher octave than normal.

He tilted his head toward me and smiled, slightly raising his eyebrows. He was using his charming smile. *On me.* "Well, this is a momentous occasion Taden." He winked at me.

"What's the occasion?"

"Our first all-nighter," he interjected. "This means we are making real progress now. All nighters are serious business. I'm honored to be pulling one with you, the mother of time travel! That in itself is a celebration," he finished, beaming from ear to ear. He seemed so genuinely proud of that night I had to fully accept that yes, indeed, it *was* a celebration.

As we ate the hummus and tabbouleh with chicken shawarma and began drinking the bottle of Pinot Noir out of paper cups, the mood of the space between us shifted. We were sharing personal stories and laughing, in fits, at each other's jokes. His were *way* funnier than mine. I'm pretty sure he was more so laughing at my pathetic attempts to be funny than at the jokes themselves.

I was beginning to feel swirly so I decided to slow down with the wine. Marius was much closer to me than he was when we started eating. I hadn't even noticed him move toward me. Or wait. *Had I moved closer to him?* Either way, I was suddenly aware we were very close to each other.

In almost the instant I realized this, Marius was penetrating into my eyes with his. It startled me at first because it felt like he was reading my thoughts. But, no, that was impossible. He couldn't know that I was over-analyzing the lack of space between us. Just as I was beginning to feel this moment couldn't be any heavier, the timer went off to interrupt us. "Time to do our next round of data collection," I said weakly.

I got up to move toward our task and he was there. He was there, in my space, through the entire collection process. I could feel his breath in the air and I was in knots of tension. His hands were on my arms bringing me to him, and his eyes had transfixed mine. I couldn't even think.

"Taden, I apologize if this is inappropriate," he said in a voice thick with seduction. Then, he paused for a few slow seconds that felt like an eternity. In this time I could have poked the intensity with my finger.

Finally, he continued. "I want to consume you."

I had imagined this countless times, which made me consider the possibility I was simply imagining it *again*. Unable to breathe properly, I nodded slightly, allowing for this inappropriate consumption.

"I'm going to kiss you now," he informed me, and before I could brace myself for this power exchange, his mouth was on mine and I had been completely defeated in the most dangerously exciting way. I never wanted to leave that moment.

CHAPTER 4

A correlation existed between sharing our feelings for each other and Marius lessening his respect for me when I stepped into authority over him. Where he used to show a high regard for my guidance in the processes of our work, he slowly replaced with a need to speak over me like he did one morning during a team meeting. I had planned to share my analysis of the previous weeks' data and the changes we would make moving forward.

"Looking at the outlier set here, I'm going to have us adjust the levels for these two components…" I turned to point at what I was referring to on the presentation slide behind me when Marius jumped in with his ideas.

"Don't you think we should leave these alone for another round of testing before we adjust anything? It seems like there is too much room for error here when we could be tightening up our protocol first to be sure we aren't affecting the results with human error among the different hands-on testing. I'd be more than happy to conduct all the testing for the next week using the original levels to look at those outcomes before we start making adjustments. What do you guys think?"

I hadn't yet turned from the slides I was referring to and so thankfully could hide my initial shock and dismay at his inability to let me finish my explanation before he laid out his own plan. "You make a good point Marius, let me finish these slides and you'll see that I address your concerns." I had become quite good at acknowledging his interjections while still maintaining my leadership. I wanted him to know that I found what he had to say was important and at times it meant holding back my ideas until timing was more appropriate. I hadn't even noticed these seemingly small adjustments to my interaction with him until they began to compound.

In response to giving him any direct instructions, his face would betray him with a look of impudence. I caught him side eyeing me more than I'd like to admit over the last few months. I don't recall the issue before becoming romantically involved. If his emotional response to my perceived power was a problem for him, I must not have noticed. Neither Dakotah nor Abel ever responded with evidence of irritation toward me. I paid acute attention to their body language and eye contact during each instance I exerted leadership, and in fact, my observation of this phenomenon revealed Abel and Dakotah responded to his harshness toward me with instinctive wincing and maybe embarrassment on my behalf. The dynamic bothered me deep down, though never enough (or maybe too much) to consciously address.

In the bigger picture, we had weeks of tests to conduct in order to keep momentum moving forward. There was no time for a power struggle but Marius was actually skipping some of our team meetings claiming he was too busy with the data collection to abandon it for a meeting. "It's not that big of a deal Tay, you can catch me up later," he would say as he flippantly dismissed me. The most recent one Marius opted out of was a briefing over the specifics and capabilities of the timed-release band. "It's not like I'll ever need to program the thing anyway. That's all done ahead of time here in the lab by Dakotah. As long as I have the basics, I'll be fine." He relied on me to summarize what he missed later on half-listening when I did.

In the near future, for Marius and I, there would be no more nights together at home. As insignificant as it should have been, I ached with longing to share a bed with him again. Even on the days when the stress and workload was overwhelming at best, I could look forward to cozying myself in his arms within the comfort of our bed. But that time was gone, and its absence should've been inconsequential to me with the biggest most foundational moment of my life on the horizon.

My first order of business was to task Abel with a schedule that would output our team's maximum time on task.

"Abel, thank you for arranging this schedule, considering everyone's needs and making the time frames work sufficiently. Put me in the schedule as much as possible. I don't want to have any more than six hours of time blocked off for sleep each scheduled day, and like I said, I intend to be here even for that. Everyone else can work a rotation that feels appropriate to them."

"I agree with Taden on this," Marius stated. "Put me on the same schedule arrangement. If it's easier for you to set up, put us on the same time blocks." I smiled at the thought that Marius was missing me as much as I had been missing him and wanted to share as much time with me here as he could. "She's right Abel, you are excellent at a schedule if nothing else."

His last remark seemed meant as an insult instead of the compliment I intended. As expected, Abel's response was both tempered and measured. First, a warning look, for Marius to understand he was overstepping, then a controlled response acknowledging Marius's desired work schedule by noting his request in the computer. Later, my amusement escaped with a chuckle to see on the final schedule, Abel had not slated Marius and I together for several weeks. But, my initial entertainment faded as I realized this meant I wouldn't be seeing much of him for the next few weeks and I already regretted not creating the schedule myself. The scheduling drama revealed relationship tension between the guys, growing even more strained than my romance with Marius as we thrust forward.

On one particular all nighter, after Marius had left to sleep in his office, Dakotah arrived to start her shift. The two of us talked honestly about being on the verge of this scientific advance and not getting to tell anyone about it. We really only had each other to share with, if we didn't include the two bickering men on our team. But we had been so busy working, Dakotah and I didn't even get to talk to *each other* anymore.

So, between data collection and constant monitoring that night, we carved out an overdue venting session covering just about every topic imaginable. However, when I steered the conversation onto Marius, Dakotah was hesitant to say much else. My natural curiosity peaked, so I circled back around the Marius topic a few times until she revealed to me her distrust of him. "Taden, you cannot possibly think that he shows you respect. In the last week, he has mansplained at least a handful of times. When's the last time you made a decision that he hasn't questioned? Anytime we make plans to go out for a drink, he gives you the third degree about where we're going and how long we're staying not to mention he's messaging you the entire time we are out. Haven't you at least noticed how he's been treating Abel anytime he interacts with you lately? The man is basically working at controlling you.

Meanwhile, he doesn't tell you anything about his friends or his family. He's constantly on his phone but who is he talking to? Do you know? Where is he when you're working and he's not? Does he tell you?"

It was difficult for me to listen openly, and I fought urges to defend him as well as to give irritated responses toward her. Most of what she was referring to I knew about already, but had worked so hard to ignore. In the end, I reminded myself why Dakotah was on my team in the first place—because I trusted her motives and actions. She had always given me every reason to.

Not only that, she had become my personal cheerleader, handing out encouragement at the times I needed it most. Dakotah was genuinely proud to be working with me *and* for me. I appreciated that about her knowing that I could've ended up with a woman on my team who would have prioritized competition with me over supporting me.

Plenty of times, she provided desperately-needed research or evidence to move us forward. She was the one who devised a timed-release version of my serum injections. Originally, I had planned for time travelers to self-administer their injection that would move them through time. Her foresight of scenarios where self-injections could be risky or even impossible stimulated the brilliant solution to preemptively solve any such problematic scenario with the concept of timed-release injections.

I firmly believed she legitimately had just as much of a right to be our leader as me, yet she never questioned my authority. If she became angry, it was righteous and directed appropriately toward injustice, carelessness, or matters impeding progress. Dakotah wasn't manipulative with her truth about Marius.

"I've come up with a plan to encrypt our data. This way no one but you and I can decipher it. With this safety net in place, we can prevent our work from being hacked or stolen."

I wonder how long I stared into her bold eyes before I responded. I was captivated by the courage and vulnerability she owned to tell me about her reservations regarding the man I had grown to love over the last several years, and then how this had inspired her to create a tangible solution.

"Look, I know what I've said has been hard to hear." She waited for me to show her approval before cautiously moving forward. I smiled and nodded. "While, yes, Marius *is* the reason I came up with the idea to data cipher, it would still be an important move for us even if I didn't have a trust issue with him. We have to safeguard our discoveries from anyone else that might find out we have time travel. I mean, Taden, our freaking country is in the middle of a tyranny. Imagine what The Reckoners could do with time travel. Can you imagine anything worse? Because I can't."

She made absolute sense and this is what I loved most about her. There was no possible scenario in which I would refuse this idea. In fact, if I was going to be honest with myself, the feelings I was having weren't about Marius at all. I was truly disappointed in myself. *How had I not thought of this? Why was this not established protocol from the beginning?* My answer was sickening: my priorities had become more tied to Marius than my work. I didn't even see it happening before me. How many times had I stayed silent when he spoke over me? That wasn't who I was. How many decisions did I make considering what he wanted me to do rather than my own instincts? I didn't operate like this. But somehow, somewhere along the way, I had shifted into this role with him. Here I stood with a major oversight having been made leaving our technology vulnerable. I felt ashamed of myself.

I'll admit there was still some guilt about keeping him (and Abel) from being able to decipher the data. Ultimately, I believed my gut instinct was the right way to go.

"You're right Dakotah. I one hundred percent agree this is necessary. Thank God you thought of it and brought it to me. It'll be hard to explain to the guys why only you and I are able to decode all of our data, though."

I was still trying to get Marius in on this even though I knew in my heart Dakotah was right. *Why was I making this so difficult for her?* I had to stop fighting for him.

"You know what?" I said, "Never mind. You are right. I'm sorry I keep bringing him back into this. I heard what you've said and it's the right move. I'll share the plan with them tomorrow."

The next day, I told the team about my decision at our morning meeting before we switched shifts over. A cold sweat broke through the crown of my forehead and the familiar sensation of blood rushed to my cheeks. I felt nauseated by my nerves, but was certain that none of them could tell. It was easier to do moments like this with a hard exterior.

"As this crisis has been unfolding, we have all become tense about the prospect of our research getting stolen from us. The Patriots agree that we need to have safety measures in place for such a situation. To address this concern, last night, Dakotah and I developed a cipher for all of our measurable data. The part of this I regret to share is that Danika agrees we should keep the cypher system for the data known to only the two of us who created it."

Informing the guys we had effectively cut them out of the intel was probably the hardest news I ever had to deliver to them. In response, Marius looked in my direction with nothing discernible on his face. He didn't look angry or upset, but he also didn't look supportive or understanding. The man didn't say a word or reveal an expression to give himself away. He sat completely still, almost frozen. I could imagine him playing a mean game of poker. That is, until Abel began to speak.

"It really is the right move Taden," Abel said. He smiled at me with a vote of confidence that I hadn't even realized I needed.

As if breaking his trance, Abel's voice triggered Marius to return to his coffee, giving the intentional impression of disregard for what Abel had to say.

"Thank you. It means a lot to have your support on this." Between my nerves about telling them this new plan and worrying about what Marius was thinking, I couldn't force a smile back for Abel. I could barely even hold his eye contact. Within his next breath, Abel had turned his attention onto Dakotah.

"Nice work D.K., I'm really impressed. Looks like you're leading the scoreboard now, eh? Although, this means we do need to make some scheduling adjustments so that either Taden or Dakotah will be in the lab at all times from this point on, since both of you will be the only two who can encrypt the data."

Dakotah chimed in, "That won't be necessary. We can keep the schedule as is. Taden and I have created a computer program that will translate into our cipher after entering the data as we normally would."

I kept glancing at Marius hoping he wasn't upset with me. He still hadn't said anything but I noticed he was clenching his jaw now. I didn't feel like that was a good sign.

Abel followed up again, confirming we were making the right move. I side smiled because I couldn't honestly accept his compliment when I felt like such a jerk about it.

The exhaustion from my night shift followed by our emotionally draining team meeting was beginning to take a toll on my body. Successive yawns escaping from my mouth felt like a free pass for me to leave and go get some sleep, but to my surprise, Abel had his own agenda to address. He turned back from Dakotah to me and spoke my name with an authority I wasn't used to him using. It was surprising enough that halfway through a yawn, I shut my mouth.

"With human travel so close to being ready *and* our mission suddenly a higher level of safety risk, I must demand that you start physical training sessions. I've *also* spoken to Danika about safety." He sort of tilted his head down and looked up at me. He too had been planning above the team to keep things safe. "I told her I would make sure it was handled and that you would be ready by launch day. Taden, you *do* need this training in case you find yourself in any combat situations."

I laughed. "I don't see why I need to be trained in combat. I'm simply going on the missions as the scientist who will be sure the real combat soldiers do not get stuck in the past." Attempting to persuade him otherwise wasn't successful. It was clear he wasn't going to accept a no from me and also, he did say that Danika had ordered me to train at his insistence.

Time travel was my inception and there was no way I would not be seeing the fruition of it on the ground floor. In my daydreams as far back as I could recall, I've seen myself as 'the first man on the moon' of time travel. I hadn't been driven to discover this technology so that someone else could test it out. It was always going to be me out there. I wanted this. If refusing to be adequately trained to defend myself might jeopardize my spot as the one to lead this then I would concede to the training.

Admitting my defeat, I gave in. "Okay. Okay. Sure, I'll spend time I do not have learning how to throw a punch or whatever. Thank you for always looking out, Abel." He was displeased at my snippy response and really, he didn't deserve it. I was taking my stress about Marius out on him. Guilt settled in right away, followed by my apology. "Abel, I'm sorry. I'm tired. I do appreciate you and you're right. Set it up." He smiled warmly letting me off the hook for being surly once again.

The unexpected twist was finding out Abel himself would be training me. I had no idea my friend was highly knowledgeable in combat training. He showed me how to get out of several holds from an attacker, had me sparring with him in boxing gloves, and taught me a few ways to permanently injure someone before they could harm me. After the first session, we were walking back, laughing at the whole event, "Okay, Abel, spill it. I *know* your history. I researched you when I hired you onto this team. So, where did you pick up these skills?"

He raised his eyebrows. "You think you know everything there is to know about me, don't you? There are things you don't know, Taden. Things that would shock you."

He cracked a smile, and I snorted at his sarcasm. We both belly laughed at the joking back and forth.

It felt rejuvenating to have some fun together like we used to back at Penn, when we were simply college kids. I couldn't help but think about what he had said, though. Some truth had to be laced in, even if he was joking. He did have to learn those self-defense skills from somewhere. Later, I would look over his file again to see if I could figure out where. It did occur to me that I could just persist in asking him, but he didn't seem like he was going to give that information up easily. No matter. I enjoyed the prospect of an investigation.

A few nights after, on one of the rare shifts where Marius and I were alone in the lab, a tightly-wound tension still lingered between us. Our power struggle was crushing my soul. All I wanted was for us to enjoy this time together on the cusp of something extraordinary we had both worked so hard to achieve.

Spooling the tension this particular evening was the fact that Abel wouldn't leave when his shift was up. After I pressed him to go, promising we would all still be here when he got back, he finally agreed to leave. But before he did, he had some concerns to get off his chest.

"I'm worried about how tired you are. Also, I know there is weirdness between you and Marius. We all know. I don't want his issues to interfere with your work. I should be here if you need a break. Trust me, I'm only half as tired as you are at this point."

His confessions were making me nervous Marius would overhear. It wasn't like Abel cared to be discreet. Partly, I wondered if he wasn't *trying* to instigate a fight with Marius. I kept looking over my shoulder to be sure Marius wasn't within earshot.

"Okay. Time to go," I said, shooing him out.

"I'll settle for going to my office for the night, but you have to promise you'll wake me if you could use a break, even if it's just from Marius," he said, pinching his face with irritation at his name. "Don't be afraid to give him an uppercut if he deserves one either, Taden."

He winked at me as he demonstrated his recommended punching jab in the air. I gave him a sarcastic smile for his verbal assault on my boyfriend before I turned away and joined Marius in the lab.

Finally alone, Marius eventually began to talk to me. "I'm worried about you. I know you want to be our first human test, but I should be going with you to make sure you're safe. Abel's plan is for you to defend yourself, but I don't think you could really protect yourself against these kinds of people just from a few training sessions. If anything bad might happen to you, I should be there."

Marius was waving the white flag on our silent battle, so I let my guard back down for him. Before long, he shared a full plan devised for the two of us. "We should go back to the week that your mom died." Instinctively, I choked at his boldness and blinked in confusion. He went on to explain his reasoning. "If we do this, you can address the moments that led to the regret you have carried all of these years. Swipe your future clear of your pain and repentance instead of letting those feelings continue to fester all these years later. You have sacrificed your life for our government to have time travel. You could die. You should at least get one benefit for yourself out of this, Taden."

His plan was something I had wanted more than anything for so long. Secretly, it had been my motivation all along: to go back to that night and tell my fifteen-year-old self to get off the bike and go back home. Plus, if I could get those drugs out of the house, Ruth never would've taken them.

If it was questionable earlier, it wasn't now. Marius loved me. Only love could have led him to this plan. My whole-hearted happiness was his intention. Filled with relief that he still cared after the distance the last few weeks had wedged between us, I wrapped my arms around his neck and kissed him. The familiar sensation of warmth and pressure between our lips and his hands around the small of my back calmed my mind.

However, Marius loving me wasn't my main priority anymore. At this point, I had my mind solely focused on one thing: saving Ruth. I would do anything to rectify letting her down. If going back to my mom endangered her at all, I wouldn't do it.

CHAPTER 5

After many mentally and physically draining, yet somehow never long enough days followed by never-ending, lonesome nights full of focused testing, we finally succeeded in sending multi-cellular organisms back for steady stretches of time. The thrill from this milestone graduated when we moved on to sending back plants, then bugs shortly thereafter. The team was losing it. Our minds were numb with exhaustion and anticipation.

One eventful evening that had stolen another day from our work pushed us into overdrive. Abel arrived for his shift clearing his throat to get everyone's attention. I heard him, but didn't look up from the plant and insect data I was analyzing. He cleared his throat again, much louder. My eyes left their task without any other muscle moving from its duty. There he stood, with an air of satisfaction, raising high a small metal cage housing a furry, gray rat.

With the cage lifted up, he tilted his head in a bow and proclaimed, "My lady Bennett, I present you with Stephen Hawking, your time traveler." I hadn't intended to go beyond insects until we had repeated our test at least a thousand more times, but everyone else was bugging me to move on already. Fear of failure was most likely the culprit. Abel knew me well enough to know it was time.

Marius looked at Abel with a smile none of us had seen in months and nodded in agreement. "Stephen, Man, we have been waiting our whole lives for you to show up."

Dakotah rushed to the cage, putting her index finger inside to pet the rat's fur, her voice taken over by baby talk. "Such a cute little time traveler you are. Are you ready to move faster than the speed of light cutie?"

We sent Stephen back that night. Our confidence boosted and our next goal was retrieving him using Dakotah's timed-release injection of the serum. We devised a band worn on the upper arm so that it could be hidden under our clothing. The band was also a way to monitor our heart rate and blood pressure, among other important aspects. We had to attach it like a collar around Stephen, which meant the injection would be inserted at the base of his neck.

I held on tight to Marius. Everything was hanging on this outcome. If we could get Stephen Hawking back to the present with no health risks, repeatedly, we were ready to plan for the first human trip. Which meant it was almost time for me to travel.

The Patriot Party bigwigs, Bernard, Joseph, and Danika, returned to establish the guidelines for these trips back. On my first trip, I would only be gone for a few minutes, just long enough for me to go, have Dakotah gather my vitals, and test out the timed-release band's ability to send me back. I alone would be going on this trip since it wouldn't require any other dangerous encounters beyond testing the process of time travel. Once we had obtained successful data, the plan would be to increase the time I spent in the past each visit I made.

The hours before my first trip back in time, I sat alone in my office staring at the adjacent wall letting myself feel the moment wash over me. Swelling with pride that I had finally made it to this point, it still didn't seem possible after this day, I would forever become the scientist who discovered time travel. A mix of excitement and anxiety kept me still. Mentally, I ran through all of the diagnostic testing that would be processed during the brief minutes I would be gone. In my hands I held the timed-release band. My thumb repeatedly passed across the screen that would be programmed to bring me back. This band had become the most symbolic element of the whole process to me. A tangible item that could be used to represent time travel in my mind. After a few steadying deep breaths, rising slowly from my chair, I used the momentum to carry me to the lab. My team and the Patriots were waiting with their own level of eager nervousness. The lab had been decorated with streamers and balloons which caused me to beam with a proud smile. Dr. Pasterski was present as well to celebrate the ceremonial first trip back. "My girl, I have waited for this day since I first took you under my wing. I couldn't be any more proud of you than if you were my own daughter. How do you feel?"

I kept the foolish grin plastered across my face and it was all Dr. Pasterski needed to know how I felt. She gave me a little squeeze before I assumed the protocol for beginning the big event. Dakotah took the timed-release band from me to program all of the tracking as she tapped across her keyboard. When satisfied her applications were running accurately, she returned to wrap it around my upper arm. In the cheesiest of launch moments, Abel began a countdown from ten. Dakotah was ready to press the launch button on her keyboard and I locked eyes with Marius. All the years and planning couldn't prepare me for what pulling apart and coming back together at a molecular level feels like. It is akin to waking abruptly from anesthesia; one minute counting backward for the good doctor, the next rapidly gaining awareness and time has elapsed beyond comprehension. Both feel harsh to the system, causing nausea and unjustified emotional overflow. By the time I could grasp what was reality my injection to return home was released into my arm. Everyone was waiting in anticipation for my return back to the present. As soon as they saw me, the relief and delight to pass over each person's face followed by fervent clapping and cheering made me feel like I had accomplished something of greatness and I had.

When it was time for a more substantial trip to expand how long I stayed in the past, we aimed for me to go back one year. From the few quick trips already made, we discovered that wherever I jump time from in the present is where I arrive in the past. If I left from the lab, I would arrive at the lab. To continue testing this theory out, I would leave from different locations within our workspace. This time I was to leave from my office. After a few minutes of acclimation looking around, it struck me as funny how much can change in a person's life in such a short amount of time. A year ago, I didn't have any framed photos filled with pictures of Marius and I together on my desk as we had just started our whirlwind romance and my piles were much smaller than they had grown to since. I winced at the fluorescent lighting that I had forgotten I changed in favor of more natural lighting to reduce headaches in the last year. Once I felt grounded, I left my office toward the lab. There, I saw Marius alone, working but behaving suspiciously. He was quickly writing something down and glancing around nefariously. This was not Marius's process. He generally carried himself with an air of importance that didn't acknowledge whether others approved of what he was doing. He certainly never rushed.

His jumpy response when I walked into the room confirmed my observations. It was like he had just been caught red-handed. He wasn't even aware that I was not Taden from the present. I have to admit it stung a tiny bit to realize he noticed so little of me that to see a version of myself a year older did not stand out to him in any way. At the very least, he must have already seen me (from the past) that day wearing something else. My hairstyle had changed pretty drastically since then too.

"Do you notice anything different about me?" He continued to look distractedly down at his notes, ignoring my question.

"Hmm?"

"Marius, look at me." I stood in front of him with my hands braced on my hips waiting for him to stop ignoring me. Once he looked up, I continued. "Do I look different?"

"I don't know. Did you get your hair done or something?"

"Well, yeah, my hair is different. But, really look at me. Do I look older to you?"

"Taden, what is this? I'm really busy. I need to get this work done."

"I'm time traveling Marius. For real. I'm here from a year in the future. This is my first trip lasting over ten minutes but I don't have a lot of time left before I go back."

He took an annoyed inhale and rolled his eyes at me. "Listen. I have a lot of work to do here. It's a funny bit though babe. I just don't have time for jokes right now."

In an attempt to distract myself from a wounded ego, I reached for the notebook he was writing in to see what he was working on. "What are you working on?" It was clear he was hiding something from me.

He ripped the paper back, and asked in an accusatory tone, "What are you doing, Tay? I'm trying to get some work done here!"

In a guttural instinct of self-preservation I turned and stormed out of the room. Almost as quickly as I stormed off, I realized I should be treated better by the man who loves me but especially from one of my subordinates. I turned on my heels, about to return and confront Marius, but the timed-release of the serum started to flow throughout my body.

It was still amazing to me how quickly it took over. I disintegrated out of that time and rematerialized in the future. The way Marius's eyes lit up as he held his arms out for me upon my return back to the present almost made me forget that I was a little hurt *and* suspiciously curious about what had just happened between us in the past.

The Patriots were pleased with the results as well. Danika was smiling at me like I was a famous celebrity. Not a trace of her hard-ass caricature lived in those brief moments. They remained present while Dakotah recorded every detail I felt and observed during my trip to the past, then collected all my vitals and blood work to be analyzed. Afterward, they arranged for a meeting the following morning with soldiers to plan the rest of our sequence for dismantling The Reckoning.

My self-defense classes were to continue every evening throughout the process. To my surprise, my non-athletic self was becoming more and more proficient, and confident as well. I didn't expect the internal side effects. I was also spending more one-on-one time with Abel than normal, which was leading Marius to make snide comments on a regular basis.

"Here they are, the Kung Fu Fighters," or, "Are you sure you have time to meet me for dinner? I thought you had a date with Abel tonight." I did expect it would bother Marius at some level, since he liked to be the center of my attention. I could understand how it was difficult for him to feel overlooked, night after night. However, the way he handled his feelings didn't make me want to spend more time with him; in fact, I could recognize myself filling time with work when I could've made arrangements to be with him. It wasn't that I didn't want to spend that time with him. I just couldn't manage my hurt feelings from his and there was so much to get done at work. I figured everything would get back to normal after we completed this mission.

I would need a team member to travel with me on the next few trips in order to perfect any issues before the launch of the entire Patriot Party's battalion. Dakotah was immediately ruled out because her role back at the lab depended solely on her. As a result, it came down to Abel or Marius.

Marius's jolting plan revealed to me in our "make peace" conversation a few weeks back was still in the front of my thoughts. I swore to him my secrecy on the matter and kept my promise, but damn if I didn't need to talk this out with someone.

Danika wanted my travel companion to be Abel. He had given quite a persuasive presentation of why he should go as my companion, including his combat background. Dr. Pasterski was asked to stay for the meeting and put her vote into the hat, which not surprising was also Abel. She had been the one to recommend him for this team to begin with.

Abel's presentation to the team was first. He shared an outline for his tactical plans and basic technology protocol in several 'what if' scenarios. "If Marius accompanies Taden in this time travel test, I'm sure he will have her best interest at heart and will do all in his power to keep her safe," Abel said. "I have to suggest, though, I am more qualified to offer the safety of Taden for this situation. I am a trained and active soldier."

I could not hide the shock on my face. I never even considered or suspected for that matter. How on Earth was he active with the military, yet working on time travel with me? Was I his assignment?

Dakotah refrained from casting a vote but locked eyes with me, knowing I would be able to read her mind. I also felt Marius looking at me as he gave his impassioned presentation of why *he* should go. He made it clear that he was concerned for my safety and would be solely focused on bringing me back. "From the day that I walked into these offices and began working alongside Dr. Taden Barrett, I knew she was a living legend. That she would be the one who would solve the theory of time travel. That she was right on the cusp of the most amazing discovery of our lifetime. Not only that, she is an amazing person with a soul that shines through darkness. It would be the greatest honor of my life to go with her in time travel and offer her support and protection if and when needed." It was a moving speech, and I loved every word of it. I felt the emotional distance between us shrink away as he spoke.

Out of the corner of my eye, I noticed Dakotah look at Abel with impatience. My cheeks warmed in embarrassment at the silliness of even contemplating Marius over Abel in this task.

After both men did their best to convince us of their ability to act as my bodyguard, Joseph and Bernard, who were split between the two men at the beginning, had decided unanimously it should be Abel going.

My adult self had become a firm "if/then" believer. I didn't feel like I could pick Abel and still have Marius. The decision wasn't as easy as it should have been. Ultimately, I picked Marius. I couldn't bring myself to look at Abel. If I had been objective and not let my feelings for Marius interfere, it would've been a no-brainer for me. But I have this residual feeling of regret from the last time I put science over someone I loved. My mom is gone now and I can't change that but I can make sure that the people I love don't feel second to the work I love. My choice being Marius for this trip was more important than who ended up going. It was clear the majority ruled and I would be going with Abel, even though my vote was with Marius. At least the right person won, regardless of who I voted for.

Later that night, we were together back at our apartment for one of the first times in weeks. After building up the courage, I confronted Marius about the time traveled to the year before. "I need to talk to you."

"What is it, babe?"

"First, I wanted to say thank you for the lovely speech you made today about wanting to protect me." He smiled contagiously which made it difficult for me to push past and bring up how I felt. "There were some details that I left out of my debriefing with the Patriots." I led with this in order to hook him in.

"Oh?"

He looked up from his paperwork to give me his full attention. I knew this to be a short window, and I had to move swiftly to keep it. I sat down in the chair directly in front of him.

"I had a conversation with you in the past that didn't go so well," I said, choosing my words carefully. "I walked in on you doing a data collection, like I told Danika, but I didn't tell her exactly how our interaction went. I told you I was from the future, and you thought I was joking. Do you remember that?"

I could see the shock on his face to realize it actually was the future me he was talking to a year ago. I tilted my head slightly to the side, as if it would assist in my confrontational performance. He nodded to acknowledge he remembered, before looking back down at his paperwork. *Damn it*, I thought, *I lost him already*. I decided to go for the gut anyway.

"I was a little surprised you didn't notice anything different about me. But, that wasn't actually the strangest part, Marius. I reached for your notebook to check out the data collection you were recording, but you became explosive in response. I've never seen you like that. Do you remember?" I asked again, feeling like a detective conducting an interrogation.

"I do remember Taden. I felt bad about it for a few weeks after. I should have apologized to you back then but I was too ashamed at my behavior. It was a difficult time having to adjust to so little sleep and nothing but the lab. I snapped. I'm very sorry." He rose from his work, walked behind me and rubbed my shoulders. "Do you forgive me?"

Wanting to end my line of questioning, he was granted a nod, my head dropped toward the floor showing my appreciation for the neck massage. I mentally recorded, though, that when I brought up the notebook I sensed he was lying to me. I would bring that up again later.

For the moment, I changed the subject to our secret trip back in time. We wouldn't tell the Patriot Party and would do this, without anyone knowing, on our next all-nighter. We were not planning on staying for more than 24 hours. We both felt it would be enough time to see my mom, get rid of the pain medicine she had left, and return back to the minute we left from. No one would ever know we had even left. But what about Ruth? I couldn't shake the feeling that I should wait until I knew she was safe before I used any time for my own desires.

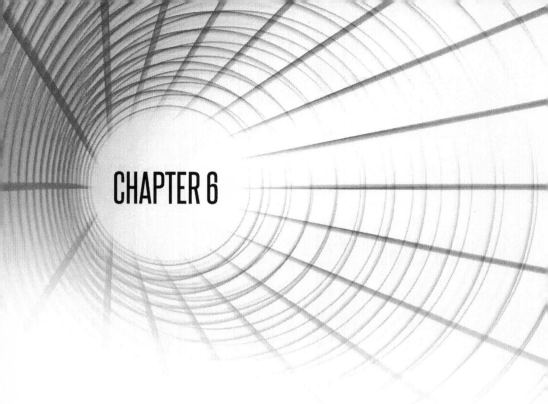

CHAPTER 6

I woke up strapped to a bed, alone in a room that appeared to be in a hospital. I had no memory of arriving here. In fact, the last thing I did remember was standing next to Marius in the lab, getting situated to travel back in time. Lying here restrained to a bed, I frantically scoured the room with my eyes trying to figure out where I was. The groggy feeling of waking from a drug-induced sleep added to my confusion and fear.

"Where am I? Why am I here? Why do you have me strapped to this bed? What is happening? I work for the government! They will not allow this!"

No one was listening. If anyone could even hear me, they were not responding. I screamed to no reply for a long time.

Eventually, a nurse granted his presence in my room but didn't talk to me. He was covered in blue scrubs from head to toe, mask and all. I was unable to see any features of the individual, and he did not even so much as look in my direction busy with arranging medical equipment. "Hello. Can you please tell me what I'm doing here? Can you hear me? Why am I strapped to this bed?" My questions fell on deaf ears. Then others came into the room, read my vitals, and left. To each new person that entered, I launched the same line of questions and none responded.

It occurred to me that maybe I had been here before. I couldn't quite place when or why, but the room seemed familiar and the eyes of my captors also gave me a feeling of déjà vu. I decided to change my script.

"I know you! I know this place! What do you want from me?"

As soon as I said this out loud, I knew. I had figured out time travel, the means to the biggest science question in the world. Abel tried to get me to understand I'd be at risk, but I just blew it off as nonsense. I needed to figure out who was trying to get this answer from me. *Why weren't they asking me for what they wanted to know? Why was I strapped to this bed? What had they done with Marius? Was he okay?*

In the midst of sorting out my predicament, a nurse appeared and stuck a needle into my arm causing me to become disoriented. As my eyes grew heavy from the drug she pushed into my veins, Marius walked into the room wearing a blue uniform matching the other medical staff. He talked quietly to another uniformed woman. For certain, I was losing my mind. "Marius...?"

The next time I was conscious, it was not clear how much time had passed. Marius was still in the room with me and I anxiously pulled at my arms, still strapped to the bed. He turned to me to see that I was awake and cleared his throat before he spoke to me.

"Ms. Barrett. I'm happy to find that you are well rested. How are you feeling? You have been very upset and we have done what we can to help you relax."

"Marius! Where are we? What is going on?" I begged him to explain.

"Ms. Barrett, you seem to be confused about who you are. You have been a patient of mine, here at this institution for several years. Recently, you seem to have had some intense delusions about yourself, which are leading you to become extremely upset." He stopped for a brief second as I stifled a laugh, assuming he was joking, but then he continued without a trace of a smile. "You are claiming to be a scientist who has discovered time travel to save the country. First and foremost, we are working to calm you down so that you may share with me what's on your mind. Can you relax, Ms. Barrett?"

As I stared at him, the laugh smothered out of my throat to be replaced with a mixture of disgust, confusion, and a bit of terror. Once I realized I had been holding my breath, a deep gasp of air was welcomed too quickly into my lungs.

"Marius, you want me to *relax?* Have you lost your mind? You have me strapped to a bed and are telling me a ridiculous story!"

He became irritated with my response, sharply exhaling in my direction. "Well, Ms. Barrett," he began tersely.

But, I interrupted him. "STOP calling me 'Ms. Barrett!'"

This time he did smile, ever so slightly (I almost missed it) and a little crooked.

He again paused to regain his composure, then continued, "As I was saying, if you can't calm yourself down, we will not be able to discuss what has been triggering these ideas in your mind. Your mother was just here to visit, while you were asleep. She is very concerned about you. She doesn't look well, Ms. Bar...I mean Taden. It would be of benefit to her health if you could manage to calm down."

At this, I was dumbfounded. My mother? What the hell was going on?! "Marius, why are you saying this to me?"

He did not answer, but a darkness fell upon his eyes. It was stunning to the point that I couldn't seem to find my voice.

"You're *scaring* me," I whispered in fear.

At that, he got up and briskly left the room.

Every bit of energy and willpower were spent focusing on the details to figure this mess out. This is my area of expertise: collecting details and solving the puzzle. This place was familiar, but why? I was almost certain I had been in this room before. Marius said I was a patient here for years. *Did he mean I had been unconscious for years? In a coma for some reason? What in God's name would cause Marius to act as if my mom was still alive and, even worse, that she was next to my side while I slept only hours ago? If my mom was alive, had I already gone back into the past? Is that where we were?*

The only logical explanation was that I must have gone back into the past with Marius. The last thing I remembered was meeting him in the lab for our subterfuge overnight shift together. We were making preparations to travel back to the week my mom died. I don't recall any details about the actual travel, though. Maybe our trip had gone wrong and had something to do with me being unconscious at this...hospital?

Marius called this place an institution. *A mental hospital?* It would be understandable, if the average person heard me discuss time travel. However, I had not spoken a word on the topic to anyone outside of the Patriot Party besides Ruth. Could she have told someone? She wouldn't ever have done that. Maybe she was followed by the people who had detained her, and they nabbed me through tailing her. None of those theories helped me explain the Marius quandary. *Why was he acting as if I'm mentally unstable?* We are *together,* he is a part of my time travel team, I *know* him, and he knows me better than anyone.

In pursuit of solving my predicament, I decided to entertain Marius's story, the one where I was delusional. If this wasn't the past, and my mom was still alive, then I would have to have been making the rest of my life up in my head. The story Marius presented to me was more than difficult to accept—it was nonsensical. His words settled into my brain like poison, but I resisted his version of reality.

It felt like hours passed before Marius returned. This time, he wheeled in a television small enough to sit atop a cart. It was an old and obsolete model, similar to the ones I recognized from my childhood.

"How are you feeling? It seems you have taken my advice, calmed down a bit and returned your blood pressure to normal." Marius stood next to my bed, reading the monitor's measurements. I wanted to say something sarcastic to him about how doctor-like he appeared, but he interrupted my biting remark with more doctor jargon. "How is your heart rate? Shall we take a listen?"

He turned toward me with a stethoscope in his hand, and I muttered something along the lines of, "Touch me and die."

He responded with a slight chuckle. Even though I was crazy, he still found me entertaining at least.

"Alright Ms. Taden, I will keep my distance." He put his hand up to demonstrate he intended no harm, and backed away from listening to my broken heart. "I want you to feel comfortable, so I won't do anything to put you at unease. Are you chilly, would you like another blanket?" I stared at him in disbelief. He continued as if he hadn't noticed my mistrust. "You haven't eaten all day. I would like to have a short session with you while your meal is being prepared. Will that be alright?"

My staredown did not break to respond but I scrunched up my forehead and furrowed my eyebrows to communicate my disapproval. I still could not figure out the angle he was after, or if he was just playing an elaborate practical joke of which I would *never* forgive him for.

"Right, well, since you are not objecting, I assume your consent to continue. Can you tell me what you are doing here, Ms. Taden?"

"I should be asking *you* why I am here shouldn't I, *Doctor Touma?*" My words were filled with enough contempt to choke the air from his breath; I remained deadlocked in a staredown.

"Sure, I can try to explain to you why you are here. Much of it may be difficult to listen to, so please let me know if you want me to stop at any time. Would you like a glass of water before I begin?" I raised my restrained arms to suggest the question, *how would I even drink it?* "I can undo one of your restraints if you would like to have a glass of water," he replied to my nonverbal question.

Feeling dehydrated, I agreed to the water but remained steadfast and *refused* to seem at all grateful or appreciative of his gesture to make me feel comfortable. As he removed my left arm restraint, my brain immediately began to plot how I would get the other arm and leg restraints off and get the hell out of there. I was considering a few moves Abel taught me in self defense classes.

Like he was reading my mind, Marius broke my train of thought. "There's no sense in trying to get free from your bed or this room, Ms. Taden. The door is locked from the outside. If you did happen to undo your restraints and leave through the door, you would find an entirely new set of challenges. Do you understand what I'm saying?" A condescending pause followed before he continued with his doctorly advice, "You could do yourself a much greater good to put your energy into working through the issues you are holding onto in your mind."

He was patronizing me, and I was enraged. Having seen him talk to just about everyone we knew this way at one time or another, it was the first time he had ever talked to *me* this way. My heart was constricted, leading to insufficient blood flow and acute chest pain. Fantastic—he had seemingly kidnapped me but it hurt my *feelings* when I realized he was disengaged from me, heartbroken he didn't love me anymore.

Once Marius was confident I would not be attempting a heroine move to escape, he walked over to the sink and filled a cup of water for me. Gulping it down, I watched him slickly settle back on his stool. Like a practiced dance number, he stretched his right leg forward onto the heel while simultaneously pulling his left leg behind him and leaning his body backward. *Why did every move he made come across seamlessly?*

With his arms folded across his chest, he looked first in the direction of the television he brought into the room and then back at me, taking great care to avoid looking right into my eyes. Abnormal behavior, for the typically charming Marius.

A distance existed between us, both physical and emotional. He was *light years* away from me. The space was cold and strange. I didn't know how to read him anymore. His facial expressions and movements didn't register. They weren't a part of my Marius glossary. Simply put, he was not mine. He wasn't my love. He wasn't my friend. He wasn't my teammate. It was a torture of its own to feel that space, especially since I had come to know and yearn for his closeness like a drug.

Over the course of our relationship, I made small sacrifices with my work losing little bits of my sense of self to stand in the light of his. The rate of our relationship felt fast-paced and time intensive because we worked everyday together and then spent the evenings with each other. I became enamored with his mind and addicted to how he made me feel. It was more than easy to let Marius lead me into devotion. But now, he had shut it off. Like a switch. I couldn't understand what he was doing or why. Momentary relief came when Marius interrupted my twisted reverie with a trait I recognized.

Marius cleared his throat repeatedly, a habit of his that gave me the distinct impression he wasn't being totally sincere. It could've been just a nervous tick, but my gut instinct was to doubt him.

"Several years ago, you became a patient of mine, as a result of the emotional trauma you were undergoing in response to your mother's cancer diagnosis. Since then, you have been in my care on a weekly outpatient visitation. About a week ago, you had a psychological episode, triggered by your mother's vastly deteriorating health. She and your sister Ruth brought you to the hospital and checked you in. Yesterday, after learning your mother's prognosis of days to weeks left to live, you understandably had a full meltdown. In the midst of your incoherent emotional breakdown, you developed a story in which you are a government physicist. You say your job is to discover time travel to save our country from a terrorist attack."

His narration yielded, expecting me to say something. I remained silent but could feel his careful observation. He would get nothing from me. I was blank. None of what he said was true. Wouldn't I remember something from *yesterday*? I think I would at least recall trying to convince people that I was a scientist like he said I did. He must have thought I would believe anything he told me.

Marius took a sharp breath in, then slowly exhaled from his body all the truth and love that ever existed between us. "Also, you seem to believe that you and I are in love, which we most certainly are not." At that, he rose from his stool and re-strapped my arm restraint.

For the first time, in the light of truth, I could see clearly that Marius Touma really was an asshole.

I crumbled into tiny pieces. Tears ripped through my eyes, despite my resolve not to allow them out. It was devastating to have him take the vulnerability I had granted him access to and twist it into this other version of reality.

He stopped talking for quite awhile after his last grenade and let me lie in silence and salt as I tried to muffle my cries. Unaffected, he seemed neither upset nor pleased with my emotional release. He did not try to comfort me in any way, or show interest in agitating me any further.

After finally settling into an exhausted, tearless purgatory, he spoke again. "I understand how difficult it was for you to process all this information. If you need me to leave now so you can eat some food and regroup, I can come back later to continue our session."

I was completely defeated, but looked right into his eyes, waiting for him to return the contact. He didn't want to. It was obvious. Out of resolve, I waited him out. At last he did. It was when we looked into each other's eyes for that fleeting moment that I first began to honestly doubt myself.

I let a thought creep into my mind that I didn't immediately reject. Disbelief started to be replaced with, *what if?* What if he was telling the *truth?* What if I actually did have a mental snap because my mom was dying? Honestly, thinking about the loss of my mom made me feel crazy. It couldn't be *too* far fetched. This sort of thing happens to people when faced with traumatic experiences.

The story did add up. My mom had cancer, I identified as a scientist and had since I was a little girl. If I had been sick and, as a result, a patient of Dr. Touma for years, I could have easily developed a crush on him and designed a story in my mind that we were together.

But, I couldn't figure out where in time this must have been. *Was I an adult? Was my mom sick, then, in my adulthood?* If so, I must have had memories with her, but I couldn't think of one.

Maybe that was what Marius—Dr. Touma—was hoping to help me with during the therapy sessions he referred to. *Or was I still a teenager, and I invented all the rest of my life into the future?* If that was true, then there was no Dakotah, Abel, or Marius—at least not the version of Marius I created. I would have made all of them up in my mind. *But then, Dr. Pasterski? Was she real?* She had to be. I knew her as a child. My dad knew her. I needed to see her. We had discussed time travel countless times. She knew I wasn't crazy.

My conclusion led me to think if I was still a teenager, then my body would have evidence to prove it. I should have felt younger. I attempted to feel my skin in order to decide if I was living in a young or old shell, but because my hands were still restrained I could not properly assess how old I felt. I turned my face toward Marius to ask him if I could have a mirror so I could see myself.

I must have been in deep thought, because he had gotten up without me noticing and was powering on the television he wheeled into the room earlier. Evidently, he wanted to show me something of importance the way he was earnestly flipping through the channels. It was enough distraction for me to forget about my body theories.

We were looking at footage from surveillance cameras located throughout the institution. There were monitors in the cafeteria, several hallways, and other patient rooms with various types of equipment in them. He abruptly stopped on a monitor placed at what looked like a main exit with a parking lot behind it.

"Here we are," he said, touching the screen to enlarge the two women who were in center view. My entire body froze as I stared at 18-year-old Ruth pushing my very alive mother outside in a wheelchair. Her face swollen from steroids, a velvet hat framed her balding head, the fuzzy blanket I continued to sleep with long after she died gently hugged around her legs.

My brain triggered the sense of her smell lingering on that blanket for not nearly long enough after she was gone. She looked up at Ruth and reached her weak hand toward her for comfort. Ruth stopped and accepted this loving gesture from our dying mother.

For as long as I can remember, I'd wanted nothing more than to see my mom again, and here she was. Right then, I quit believing the alternate reality my brain had created to save me from the loss of her. My mom was here. She was not dead, and I was wasting our last moments together with this ridiculous nonsense. Not wanting to lose another precious minute, I gave everything over to Dr. Touma.

Pleading in desperation with him to let me see her. "Please! Can you get her to come back? I see now. I have created this delusion because she's dying, and I don't want to lose her, but I am losing her every second I'm here! I need to leave and be with her. Please let me out of here." The anguish rising in me replaced any heartache I was feeling at the loss of Marius just minutes before.

"Alright Ms.Taden, shhhhh." He tried to calm me again. "I promise I will be in contact with your sister as soon as I can. We will arrange for you to spend time with your mom very soon. Unfortunately, as I just told you, she was here while you were still unconscious and she needed to go home to get some rest herself. She is very weak, and it is important she take care of herself.

When she is strong enough to return, she will be here. Your mom loves you very much and has visited as often as she could this past week."

I was fully hysterical, the sobbing that broke out of my body felt like it had been locked away for years and was finally, released into the freedom it deserved. I'd never heard any human body make the noises my collapsing body made.

Dr. Touma pulled out his phone and called in a request for drugs to calm me down. Mere minutes later, he answered a knock on the door, opening it just wide enough to reach for the medicine that arrived and shut the door again.

"Ms. Taden, you have made enormous progress in this session. I am very proud of you. You need to eat some food so you can replenish your energy, but to do so, you'll first need to return to a more relaxed state. I have a sedative I am going to give you, but it is much less potent than what you've been getting. It's just enough so you can calm down to eat some food. Is that okay?"

I nodded my head in obedience choosing to accept what he was telling me whether I fully believed him or not. I was a teenager. My doctor had just figured out what was wrong with me and how to make me better. My mom was dying, and I needed to be with her. For the first time, I looked at Dr. Touma with gratitude, because I understood that he wanted to help me. I turned my arm over so that he could inject the sedative without resistance.

Instantaneously, I felt the drug do its work in my body. Each muscle let go just a little bit from its hold on the scientist, then let go of time travel, let go of The Reckoning, let go of Abel, let go of Dakotah, and finally let go of Marius. It actually felt a lot lighter not to carry the weight from my imagined life. The concept of returning to my youth where I was not in charge of everything felt underwhelming in such a dramatic way that I was overwhelmed with relief.

My breathing stabilized and it felt like the room was filled with fog, reminding me of summer mornings after a rain when the sun peeks into the sky and starts heating up the day.

Pulled from my misty meditation, a nurse noisily entered the room with my meal. Obliging, by my doctor's orders, I ate each portion of my meal. Taking my time, I chewed slowly, aware of the sensations my food brought before it traveled down to my stomach. This had to be the first time I had eaten in days. My thoughts swirled around the concept that I hadn't noticed my hunger until I started feeding it. Dr. Touma must have left the room while I was eating because he wasn't there when I looked over at his chair. After finishing the religious experience of the meal he suggested I eat, I drifted off into a state of wakeful sleep.

My mind settled onto an odd moment between Abel and me that happened back in our senior year of undergrad at UPenn. I immediately tried to dismiss it as another hallucinated memory, but it wouldn't budge from my consciousness. After wrestling it for awhile, I gave in to the memory, whether or not it was real.

 I was in the campus library, working on my physics research project, but had drifted into a daydream about my mom. I was remembering her birthday a few years before she died, when the two of us took a trip to do a literary walk of L.M. Montgomery, our favorite author.

We stayed in an antique bed and breakfast that boasted an important history for Montgomery. To our delight, other nerdy followers were also there doing the same trek through this author's world. After a day of touring and listening to various accounts of her life, all of us super fans went into the living room of the inn, laughing together as we shared our favorite works or quotes from different books she had written. My mom was sitting next to me, drinking hot chocolate on an old, scratchy couch in front of a crackling fireplace that set the tone for this cozy evening. She smiled at me, delighted with the memory we were creating, and I knew the feeling of unconditional love.

Deep into reliving this memory, someone behind me dropped a book, instantly snapping me out of L.M. Montgomery's living room and back to the school campus library.

I realized I was staring at somebody, dazed out. I've always hated it when I do this. I looked away as fast as possible, but then I realized it was Abel.

He was looking right back at me. The moment that our empty, locked gaze became aware, he beamed. Although I knew my red face betrayed me, I tried to conceal my embarrassment, so I returned his smile and gave him an awkward wave.

He must have taken that as an invitation, because he got up to approach me. I wanted to climb into a dark hole and hide. Instead, I dug deep to find my dignity and talk to him. Deciding to be honest, I mustered out, "Oh, hey. I'm sorry I was staring at you! I was fully zoned out."

I took a deep breath of relief. I hoped this was the end of the conversation. Just in case, I was about to switch this mortifying topic to the less personal topic of my physics thesis, but Abel got a word in before me.

"What were you thinking so hard about, Taden?"

The honesty of his question caught me off guard. It also cut into my pain for how much I missed my mom. My skin began to heat up again, not to mention the extra water my eyes were starting to take on. Abel stood unaffected, still gently waiting for me to respond. I took another deep breath, hoping to calm myself before I gave an answer. Again, I chose honesty as my reply.

"Oh, I was just reliving a memory."

That should've been enough information for him. Maybe it was even enough honesty to make him uncomfortable, so he wouldn't lean in so much. However, he beamed at me again, a little more this time. He leaned in even closer, definitely closer than I felt comfortable with. I knew enough about Abel at that point to know it was closer than *he* normally felt comfortable with, too.

"Don't get taken in by your past, Taden. Here, in the now, there's friendship, love, and loyalty. Be here in the now." I smiled back at him, not wanting to reveal how his words had been busy penetrating the walls I had carefully erected to feel less vulnerable to the world.

I tried to be funny to cover up the battle that was raging within, and said with sarcasm, "That's deep, Abel. You oughta get that on a card!"

He laughed, still gently, but stayed centered in our moment together.

Unfortunately, I do not remember a single word of the continued exchange after that. I checked out of the conversation to tend to my heart.

 After reliving my moment with Abel, my conclusion was that it couldn't be real. Willing myself to overcome this delusion, I repeated, "This is not a real memory. This never happened. You don't know Abel."

But no matter how much effort I put into controlling my mind, I continued to have a difficult time letting him go. How could I have such a visceral attachment to a made-up memory? I felt like I was going crazy. I realized what I was indeed doing in this mental institution, but it was beginning to feel like more than I could handle. I just wanted to be the 15-year-old girl trying to get home to her mother. Why couldn't I accept the truth?

CHAPTER 7

RUTH

My new life was coming together almost perfectly. Between my cheap apartment right outside of L.A. and the public relations gig I landed, a familiar high was pumping through my veins. In the back of my mind, I wondered if that rush of adrenaline would make me want more. My kick-ass job involved working closely with the mayoral office of Los Angeles, helping to plan and host political events. The political scene wasn't very exciting, but I certainly didn't mistake the opportunity sitting in my lap. My PR job is how I met my best friend.

The lead liaison between the governor's office and my agency was a contagiously extroverted Latina. The way she tells it, she immediately saw the lost puppy dog look in my eyes. She scooped me up and introduced me to a fresh start outside of Maryland. Eventually, the two of us, Maria and Ruth, became the hottest duo in town. I was the tiny, power-packed punch and she was the carefree, curvaceous kick. Maria worked hard and played hard. A tight work ethic had been instilled in me at youth, but ever since I faced my addiction I was a perfectionist of not enjoying life for fear of a relapse. The start of our friendship was reserved due to me holding back from any scenarios that might lead to my loss of control. Eventually, Maria confronted me about avoiding fun. My decision to open up to her about my drug addiction led to many long conversations of healing and strength. Los Angeles was a world waiting for me to discover, and Maria held onto my map containing the directions.

A few years of rocking it at event planning led me to major connections on the political ladder, along with a massive networking system which extended throughout the city. I frequently wondered what my mom would think of my life here. How proud of me she would be.

Maria was still working at the governor's office and we kept matching each other's pace in our careers. She continued to move up the chain of command as I continued to become a more prominent event planner. In the last year alone, I had landed the account with a major athletic shoe company for their employee holiday party, a 15th anniversary celebration for our local news station holding number one ratings, and a merger social event between the top two cell phone companies based out of L.A.

As our lives overlapped professionally and personally, Maria and I naturally developed an even closer bond. In some ways, I felt the lit up vacancy sign on my soul fade. It didn't take long before we moved into a modern loft together in the heart of L.A.

Then, out of nowhere, our relationship became strained. Maria was coming home agitated and acting unusually stressed out about work. I would inquire about her day and she would dismiss me in a way that felt on a deeper level like she was pushing me back. I'd ask her if I could do anything to lessen her workload and she'd tell me she had it under control. I didn't let up and kept offering my support however I could. Eventually, she confided to me that she wanted me to leave California for a few weeks and go home to Maryland.

"I just think you need to see Taden. You haven't been home in so long, and I've been incredibly busy at work. You must be lonely."

"I call bull. What is this really about?"

She didn't have any good reasons to want me to leave, but as the weeks progressed her requests for me to visit home turned to begging me to pack and leave as soon as possible.

I thought Maria was crazy, initially, but she was so persistent and emotionally distraught I finally gave in.

Since the move to L.A., I'd only been home twice. The feelings of going back were unpleasant, and avoidance was my go-to. I regularly tried not to relive memories that made me feel broken but at times it was futile.

When my Mom got ill to the point that she was bedridden, we watched the series *The Gilmore Girls*. It was my mom's favorite show. Before she had us, she used to watch it in real time as it aired every week on cable. She said she loved the show mostly because it reminded her of her relationship with her own mother. It was the happiest either she or I could be under the depressing circumstances we had been dealt with. I didn't feel quite so lonely when we watched our show together. It was easier to forget she was dying in the forty-minute window we could watch an episode.

Taden was never really there. She was missing the most important thing to ever happen in our life with our mother. Often, I would feel jealous and betrayed by her because she had somewhere else to be and she always chose to be there instead of here. My mom was dying but it felt like Taden was hardly aware of it, never mind my seeding resentment.

In one of the episodes we were watching, a main character had a heart attack and almost died, leading the other characters to address grudges they had been holding onto. My mom turned to me, reaching out her hand.

"Ruth, you know when I'm gone it's just going to be you and Taden. She doesn't know any better than to try to escape this pain. I know it's not fair to you. I know this is hard for you. You have to be the big sister and take care of her for me. Please Ruth, forgive her, and let her be a little girl for as long as she can."

I swore to my dying mother that I would take care of my sister, and even though I didn't know how to address these emotions, I wouldn't let my mom down.

We had gotten all the way to the last episode of season three on the night my mom died. The daughter in the show was giving a speech about how much she wanted to be like her mother.

What she said struck a nerve with me. My mom raised my sister and me to believe we could do anything we put our mind to. As a single mom raising two girls alone since my dad died, she showed me what that looked like by not only modeling it day to day for me, but also pointing me towards other women who had done amazing things with their lives. Every day she went to two jobs, took us girls to and from the places we needed to be while connecting in meaningful conversations with us when she could've been zoned out from exhaustion. She regularly cooked meals that we sat down and ate together when quick fast food options would've been so much easier for her. With all that she did on her own, she also created a close knit circle of women that she leaned on to help raise us. Demonstrating the strength and devotion she had within her but also the beauty that lies in community with others.

In hindsight, I was gifted with the knowledge that my mom loved me no matter what. After that love was lost, it hurt more than any physical pain I've ever known. I searched for a relief for this kind of pain. In the middle of that episode, I climbed into bed with my mom and for the last time ever, she held onto me and said her goodbye.

"Sweet Ruth, I love you."

From then on, when I felt like she was too far away from me, I would take the pain away and watch that entire episode again. I knew she was dead. I wasn't crazy. But also, I wondered if maybe she just got lost somewhere. I would look for her at the grocery store, in the faces of strangers, and in the faces of people I knew. Eventually, I realized she was really gone and all I had left now was the gaping wound in my soul. But even so, I kept looking for her in that episode of *Gilmore Girls*.

 To keep expecting Taden to come visit me was selfish, and I knew it. That prickly little feeling of guilt made me look into flights home.

Taden had no idea about the pending visit because Maria made me swear not to speak a word of it to anyone. Although I didn't get why she was so intense about this issue, I trusted her with my life. So finally, I agreed.

I tried to get Maria to come with me, but she wouldn't entertain the idea for even a second. Of course my thoughts narrated a story about our dying relationship and how obvious it was becoming that Maria wanted me gone. Instead of dwelling on it (or getting high to push it out of my mind), I made a promise to Maria I wouldn't say anything and consciously decided how fun it was going to be to surprise Taden with a visit.

My plane landed in New York on a red-eye layover. An hour into my layover, I learned my connecting flight home was cancelled, along with every other damn flight in the entire airport. It was about to become mad chaos. Not wanting to get stuck an extra day and night in New York for a flight the day after, I rushed to a rental company outside the airport.

When *it* all started, I was on my way out of New York, headed to Taden. Safe.

CHAPTER 8

On the taxi ride headed to the rental car company, I tried to call Maria to let her know I landed. I wanted to tell her about the layover and what my new plan was. The driver noticed me having trouble with my phone and nodded his head, saying, "Same with me. My phone is on the fritz. I think a satellite is down."

I smirked. "Terrific."

Standing at the counter for the rental car process felt like forever, as a result of some technology difficulties. The service representatives were trying to sort out the issue, but it appeared the computer system wasn't processing anything internet related. They ended up having to get their manager who could do the entire rental transaction on paper.

It was strange, for sure, but it wasn't like technology complications never happened in *my* office. When tech glitches transpired, it was typically best to swim with the tide. Once the tech crew could get to work on the problem, it didn't take too long getting back on track.

The only part that made me uncomfortable with the rental car process was leaving my credit card information on this archaic paper contract. This meant anyone who might find it would have the ability to commit identity theft with my account. I had no other option but to wait out this madness back at the airport if I didn't proceed with the rental contract, so I decided to take the chance and get the car.

Finally inside my rental, I turned on the radio—but only found static. Giving up, I turned it back off and attempted to set my GPS for Taden's. That signal wasn't working, either.

In general I am not a conspiracy theorist, but I was beginning to doubt all these weird happenings were coincidence. It was late afternoon by the time I finally left the rental company, and I had only eaten a muffin at the airport that morning. Feeling hungry, I stopped for lunch before starting my long journey home. Eating cut into some of that last bits of daylight I could've been on the road.

It was already a depressing, gray winter day that easily reminded me how much I hated the snow and slush persistent on the east coast this time of year. Evening hadn't even set in yet and it was beginning to get dark already. I would never know how people live with such little amounts of sunlight in their life. The car's automatic headlights went on. It felt so much later than it really was. Man, I was glad this was only meant to be a short visit. I didn't know how much of the east coast weather I would be able to take.

Not long into my drive on Grand Central Parkway, I noticed what appeared to be military trucks coming from several different directions. A prickling of fear crept up my back. My instincts kicked in, linking the unusual military presence to the odd events leading up to this point. All at once, I was sure Maria's irrational behavior to get me out of L.A. also had something to do with this chaos. Maria thought I was in a plane on my way home to Maryland. I wasn't even supposed to be in New York right now.

Panic set in. To avoid hyperventilating, I coached myself aloud.

"Breathe, Ruth. You can figure out what to do. Be calm and think."

I shut my headlights off to avoid being seen. Each time trucks approached, I turned down a neighborhood side street and waited until I could sneak back onto the main road to continue shortening the distance to Taden. The rapid darkening of the sky was never appreciated so much.

It was frightening to see so many armed vehicles spilling into the city with no apparent reason. In my whole life I have never seen anything like it and I couldn't think of any good reasons why something like this might be happening. I felt compelled to stay out of their way.

My duck and dodging attempts became more difficult when I finally got onto the open highway. What should have been a four- or five-hour drive to

Maryland turned into a much longer excursion than I could've ever imagined possible.

In the back of my mind, I stressed with the thought of daylight inevitably creeping up. All that could be covered in the dark of night was not so easily hidden in broad daylight. I did not want to be seen or to see what was happening. I felt unsafe, and the thought of seeing clearly what was actually happening made my chest thump like I was watching the killer revealed in a horror movie.

I had to find a place to stop soon. Just off an exit in a small town, I happened upon an old motel that would serve as a good place to hide out until the next nightfall when traveling would be more discreet again.

The dumpy motel looked like it had been around since my grandma was a kid. To be honest, at first glance, it didn't even appear as though it was still open for business. Zero cars were in the parking lot and it was pretty much run down in every way. I decided even if it was closed up, it would be my hide out for the day.

Pulling into the drive, I noticed a small neon light flickering, "open." Surprise surprise, the little-motel-that-could. Still, I parked my car in the back so the appearance of vacancy was given to the military moving through. I didn't know who they were or what they wanted, but I was certain about one thing: I didn't want to meet them.

I speedwalked around to the front of the motel and entered through the main office door as if I was being hunted. At the counter, I met a younger guy with piercings splattered across his face and hair dyed Kermit green.

Unexpectedly he was reading a book, which he politely put down to greet me. I didn't think that kids with nose rings read books. I imagined I was the only person who had tried to check in at all that day—maybe even the day before too. He was pretty far along in his book.

"Hi there, Ma'am. Are you looking for a room?"

"Yes, thank you."

"Where you headed? On vacation?" he continued.

"I'm actually heading home to Maryland. I was on a flight but the layover was cancelled, so I'm driving the rest of the way now. I'm *really* excited about it too."

I squeezed in a little sarcasm to appease his teen humor. With lament at my coolness attempt, he released a tiny scoff. Although I was trying to stay polite and banter with the kid, I felt a sense of urgency to disappear in a room.

"Let me see what I can do for you," he said as he got up from his book and comfy stool. He strolled over to the computer in order to reserve me a room. It had been hours since I left the airport, so I figured if his computer wasn't working, he probably would've figured that fact out by this point.

Still, I bit back the urge to smartly tell him not to count on the computer today. He wouldn't even think it was funny anyway—but then, when that was exactly what *did* happen with the computer, I stifled my disbelief and simply suggested to him the paper contract idea that the rental car company had used.

He looked at me like I was insane with the idea of booking a room at their motel with paper and pencil. I would have agreed with him in any other circumstance, but this situation was feeling more and more concerning by the minute.

He seemed to notice my state of desperation and out of what I can only assume was pity searched the drawers in the desk for some kind of contract that could be used as backup on such an occasion. As expected, he was unable to find anything.

Daily life had been computer-reliant for decades. I remember wondering, as we became more technology-dependent, what would happen if our computers ever went down.

Paper had transitioned out of use so that finding a piece of it lying around was not common. After his failed attempt, he was about to apologetically send me on my way, but I was not about to go anywhere. There was a reason I was successful in PR, and I was about to show this kid what that reason was.

I could handle most problems like a boss, and this one was not going to be the exception. In no time I had located a piece of paper from a flyer (which appeared to be years old). My plan was to use the back to create a short contract in order for me to stay in one of their crappy motel rooms. In the midst of negotiating with this guy, I found out he went by the name of Trey.

Trey was totally cool with my contract and found me both funny and inventive with my solution to his techy malfunction. I was pretty pleased with my chill factor at that point. Still, I was on a mission to disappear.

Not much later, I was hiding out in a museum-like motel room. It reminded me of the room that Lorelei stayed in when she took off on a camping trip in the revival season of *Gilmore Girls*. It smelled like a must that had not been disturbed in decades and felt like dust mites had claimed the space as their own. However, I did not feel that my situation lent to many other options, and I was relieved just to have a place to camp out.

Throughout the day, I switched between neurotically peeking through the rose-covered, pleated curtains and trying to force sleep to take me while lying on the matching, floral comforter. Neither were productive. For one, I could not sleep longer than a few minutes without nervously jumping awake at every noise. Each noise convinced me someone was trying to break into the room through the ramshackle door and take me away somewhere awful in one of those daunting army trucks. Secondly, all peering out the window did was produce a confirmation that I did, in fact, have something to be afraid of. The soldiers coming from the trucks appeared not to be part of our government. Not that I've had many interactions with many military soldiers in my lifetime but what little I knew, these people did not fit the image I had from the news or the brief passing by of a solitary uniformed soldier who might be at the same airport as me. These soldiers seemed more like terrorists with their imposing nature and the look of someone on a hunt, filling the streets like I've seen in apocalyptic movies and video games. I felt certain that either I needed to be very afraid of these soldiers or that there was some other event going on which required the resources of these soldiers to stop. Either way, I sensed something terrifying was at play.

The longest day of my life finally transitioned to evening. I snuck back to the office of the motel so I could find Trey again, see if he was also noticing what was going on out there, and hopefully get out of New York as soon as possible.

The door was locked. Disturbed at the idea that Trey might have left me here alone, I knocked and noticed him peek up from below the counter. When he saw me, he quickly shuffled to the door to unlock it and let me in. He had shut off the neon "open" sign and all of the lights in the office. It appeared he had become aware of the ominous arrival of all these armored vehicles and weapon soldiers.

"Oh hey," he greeted with what I interpreted to be relief as I made my way through the door. "My shift was supposed to end earlier today, but my coworker, Jamie, didn't show up. When I tried to call him, the phone wasn't working. I didn't feel right leaving the motel unattended while you were here, especially with the computer system not working, so I decided to hang around."

He sounded sort of robotic while he told me about his extended shift, and I suspected he had seen as much as I had. He went on to describe all the things he saw throughout the day, while he sat behind the desk. He recounted soldiers and tanks slowly but steadily trickling in ever since I checked in that morning. He told me he knew they weren't American, because of the black and red color scheme of the vehicles they were using and the red uniforms they were wearing. Traditionally, our country had been uniformed with digitally camouflage patterns and drove vehicles of the same.

I could see Trey was in shock and having a hard time processing all of it. I understood how he felt because I was a grown woman and felt it. This poor tatted-up kid was here all alone, taking in the madness. He hadn't even registered in my mind back in the room, so consumed by my own worry.

"I've been hiding under the check-in desk like a coward. I'm effing relieved that you're here and I'm not alone anymore. I wanted to go to your room but I was too freaked out to leave the office."

Leaving wasn't an option after that confession. I couldn't abandon the poor kid like that. "Dude, you're not a coward, this is some scary shit going on. You were smart to hide. What do you think I was doing all day?"

It became obvious that I wasn't going to simply drive out of New York like I had originally planned. The streets had become littered with the soldiers carrying machine guns that I first noticed from my room. They had begun patrolling the area taking posts at street corners. I hadn't seen them do anything violent to anyone but they were stopping the occasional vehicle and instructing them to park their cars and leave the area on foot. They were making their presence known and demonstrating their man power. Everyone mostly stayed out of their way gawking from the distance.

"Do you think they will leave soon? There's nothing here for them. I don't understand what they could even want here." Trey hoped but nothing suggested that was their plan.

"I know. It just doesn't seem like they are going anywhere. Come on away from the window. I bet you haven't even eaten yet today. Sit down back here with me and let's eat a little." I learned a lot about him that week. It's amazing how quickly a life-threatening situation can inspire a connection at such an accelerated pace. "Do you have any brothers or sisters?"

He chewed on some cheese crackers from the vending machine looking at me with concern in his eyes. "I do. I have two older sisters and two younger sisters. I'm the only brother in a house of girls. They were all home alone because my parents were at work when this started. I hope they're okay. I hope my parents are okay. I don't even know if they got home or stuck somewhere like us." He set his food down next to him and dropped his head.

I put my hand on his shoulder to offer some comfort. "Wow, four girls. That's a lot of women in one house. It was just women in my house too. Me, my sister and my mom. I can relate to that much estrogen." I paused, "I'm sure they're all safe." Nodding my head at him partly to console him of his worry but also to convince myself that this whole situation wasn't as scary as it seemed like it was.

A couple of days went by as we remained hidden in the office of the motel passing the time in conversation and playing card games. "So, what do you want to be when you grow up?" It's a funny question to ask a teenage boy. They seem to be already mostly grown up but after talking to one for a few minutes, it's easy to see how much of a child still lingers in the oversized body. Asking him what he wanted to be when he grew up felt like an oxymoron and it caused us both to laugh a little.

"I plan on going to college to work in hospitality. That's why I work here. To get experience working in a hotel but this run-down motel is the only place that would hire me. People don't seem to see my potential. They only see my piercings and green hair." He spoke to me with an open and honest quality I found to be unique for someone his age.

"I know what you're saying. Often, the first impression I give people is that I am a tiny fragile woman who couldn't possibly handle anything of substance, but once they get to see me in action I love proving their judgement of me wrong. Don't worry too much about what people think of you right off. Work hard and let your reputation speak for you." I felt moderately hypocritical recalling my first impression of the kid to be in line with everyone else. Based on first impressions, I made assumptions about Trey that, after engaging him in conversation, led me to quite the opposite conclusions. I was disappointed in myself for being like everyone else.

The tension of the presence of the soldiers lingered in the air despite the familiarity of comfort we had begun to develop with each other. Outside, it appeared to have become a ghost town for everyone but the soldiers. Civilians seemed to have disappeared. A few tents had been set up by the unwanted guests. They either remained outside or stayed in their vehicles from what I could see. I wasn't sure if they were going into any of the houses or buildings in the area but none of them had approached the motel at that point.

The first few days, hiding seemed like the best option until this thing blew over, but it was beginning to feel like we could be stuck here for an extended length of time, no noted violence had been observed, and so we began to plan our exit strategy. Still, I was relieved to be there in the motel with Trey instead of alone out on the road. "I don't think we should leave just yet. Maybe give it a few more days and if nothing changes then we can try to go.

Even then, dude, I think we should stick together. Who knows what's really going on out there."

"Yeah, I'm not stoked about the thought of going off on my own but I know you want to head out of New York and I gotta try to find my family. You know, get back home. See that everyone is alright. You should come with me."

"Trey, listen. You want to head deeper into this mess. I want to leave the area. I think you should come with me. Whether or not your family is safe. There's not a whole lot you can do right now." He shook his head slowly to communicate he wouldn't leave without his family.

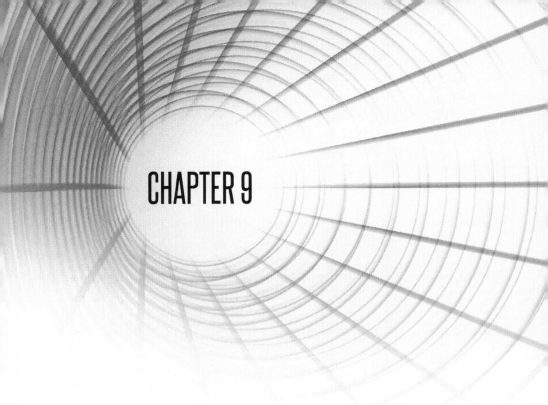

CHAPTER 9

During the days that passed, we watched with growing horror what unfolded through the window. The first shocking incident occurred in response to a middle aged man who appeared from somewhere west of the motel. He was bundled up in his winter gear to bravely approach a group of soldiers standing in the street in front of their oversized truck. Every one of the soldiers was slinging intimidating machine guns over their shoulders. In contrast, this man came bearing no weapons beyond his own courage.

"Who are you people? What are you doing in my town?" He did not waver in the face of the soldiers' dismissal. "I demand you explain yourselves!"

This time, they didn't ignore him. Instead, they shot him down in cold blood. A woman, who I assumed was his wife, ran to him from the same direction he had come from. Her screams were deafening, but before she reached her husband lying on the ground, they shot her dead too. I couldn't stop replaying the vision of tiny feathers from the man's down-filled coat floating into the cold winter air.

That couple was not the last to attempt confronting the terrorists. They were not the only ones who were cruelly killed either.

It didn't take long before the streets stayed empty of everyone *but* the terrorists. Their message had been sent loud and clear. If there was anyone else sticking around in this town, we were all hiding inside, watching from windows, praying they would not come for us.

At first, we could not figure out what they were doing here or why they were killing people. It was beyond terrifying. Our only solace was found in the hope that they were not interested in us. Trey and I decided we would be okay; they weren't going to harm us if we stayed out of their way and hidden. We did this as best as we could. Desperate to understand what was happening, though, we continued to watch and listen carefully. I watched them day after day as they walked up and down the streets, machine guns in hand. My impression was that they were starting to get bored. Their faces were hungry for a challenge.

One morning, Trey went out the back and crept along the brush on the side of the motel to listen to a group of them eating breakfast in a huddle on camping chairs they had brought. I watched from the office window, finding the very act of breathing to be difficult. *What if they saw him? Would I be watching my friend die this morning? Would they come for me next?* He was out there for what felt like hours. I continued watching with trepidation until he finally turned back, creeping through the overgrown brush toward the rear of the motel where he exited from.

The consolation I felt that he was returning to me was quickly hijacked by fright the moment he tripped over his own feet trying to be stealthy. I could not believe my eyes and a gasp left my mouth, which I muffled with the palm of my hands. Immediately and intensely, I turned my wide-eyed attention back to the soldiers' breakfast gathering. It appeared they hadn't noticed Trey's blunder. Thankfully, they were too distracted with each other. Trey wasn't tempting the fates any further and got his ass back inside the motel.

From his eavesdropping, Trey learned that these soldiers were already successful in their mission to set up posts throughout the city and monitor civilians to keep order. They were definitely not working for our government. Some references had been made about taking over the state to colonize for their people just as soon as they could get rid of the American trash. Trey heard them communicating with others over walkie talkies. Repulsively, a tally of which battalion had the most civilian kills was being accrued. They weren't here to protect us, their leaders wanted our land and were going to take it however they needed to. Maybe even, how they *wanted* to. He told me that a female soldier in the group suggested they could increase their kill number of Americans more easily if they started patrolling inside buildings. Trey said they all cracked up at her in approval. It made my abdominal muscles tighten and my blood run cold. Murdering our citizens was like collecting bonus points in this plot for power to them.

If that wasn't sickening enough, they were picking which houses and buildings they were going to raid for supplies and then set up camp in after they killed whoever was inside. From the general impression Trey took from the group, they were settling in here and while they were here, they were going to take what they wanted, whether it be food, shelter, or life.

Needless to say, our false sense of security crumpled beneath us. On the sixth day of hiding, we watched approximately five soldiers enter buildings nearby. We heard people screaming, guns firing, then silence. I have never been so terrified in all of my life. We felt like sitting ducks. Our plan was to go back to my motel room and hide in the closet, sure no one would find us there. In a hurry, we gathered food and water and slipped out the back to room three. For two days, we stayed concealed in that closet, only leaving to use the bathroom. We took turns keeping watch and sleeping. Although when it was my turn to sleep, I couldn't make it come. Mostly, we sat in silence. There was a book in the nightstand next to the bed, and I used what little bit of daylight streamed in above the curtains to read. Any noise we heard sent us into frozen fear. The kind where you can hear your heart beating like it's coming from the next room but the motel continued to be ignored and we assumed it was because of its appearance after all. Eventually, we felt safe enough to head back to the main lobby again where we had access to more comfortable survival necessities.

We couldn't stay in the motel forever, and the longer we stayed the less likely we would be getting out of this alive. Eventually, we developed a specific plan so that when we saw an opening, which took a few weeks, we could get away.

I would escape at night running through the cover of trees. Trey's plan was to escape the motel and get back home to his family. I thought his plan was pretty stupid and I didn't pretend it wasn't either. He was just overcome with worry and couldn't stop thinking about their safety. He had no intention to leave New York until he had his family with him.

While I knew how that felt, I still made an attempt to talk him into leaving with me, instead.

"If your family is safe I know for a fact they wouldn't want you to risk your life for them. We should both be going the other way, dude."

Trey looked hopeless, like he was questioning the world of its goodness and deciding there was none left. He stood his ground, unwavering, with a hope that his family was alive and safe. It was way more than I gave him credit for, even after I had spent weeks with him. All I could do for Trey at that point was hope he would at least make it home to see them alive.

On our last day together, just as the sun was setting, Trey opened up a safe underneath the registration desk to reveal a pistol.

"Are you kidding me?! This was here the whole time?!"

"I know. I know. I knew you were going to be mad about this, but hear me out. I am not comfortable using this. I've never even opened the safe until today—it's only in case of robberies. I'm not taking it. I got it out for you, Ruth. Take it with you, and get out of New York."

This kid! He was infuriating and amazing all at once. There was no way I could let him go to the showdown and not take this gun with him. Sensing our goodbyes getting closer, I ambled over and wrapped my arms around him in a big hug. He felt like the little brother I never had even though he towered me in height. With my arms around his skinny torso, I said, "I need you to take that gun and get to your family *alive*. I'm not asking you. I'm telling you." He nodded in acceptance. "Do you know how to use it?"

"I've never touched a gun before, but I had to watch a bunch of tutorials when I started working here so I could get my certification." He looked down at the ground, feeling guilty for giving in to me on this issue.

"Look, I still think you should be coming with me. But, if you aren't going to be reasonable, then you for sure have to take that gun and be ready to use it."

I turned my attention to the window and noticed that the soldiers had dispersed from their night posts. Not long after the terrorists had made claims on some houses and buildings, most of them stopped staying outside on night post. Instead, they would head back to their barracks in the evenings, leaving only a few behind to keep watch. The ones who stayed behind seemed so sure that no one was going to try anything shady that they had become lackadaisical about their night shift.

"Okay Trey, are you ready? It's time to go. Let's get out of here!" I really loved that kid, and more than anything I wished he would reconsider his family honor and just leave with me. Again, aware of my hypocrisy considering the lengths I was about to take to get to my own sister. I really just couldn't fathom letting him go out that door to what felt like certain doom.

We crept out the back, just as Trey had the morning he pretended he was a spy. We tried to make absolutely no noise until we reached the end of the parking lot. I took one last look at Trey before heading right. He went the other direction. I didn't look back. It was the only way I could let him go.

About a block into my escape route, I heard a single gunshot. It wasn't the sound of one of the machine guns that the soldiers used to snuff life out with. Just one shot. It had to be his.

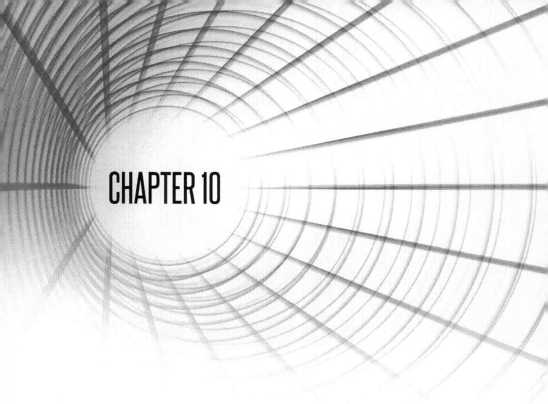

CHAPTER 10

As if pulled by a magnetic charge, I found myself walking toward the sound of the piercing gunshot. But then, I stopped remembering that I promised him I would not look back and I would stay on my own path. Burning choked my throat rising up through my face into my eyes. Using every ounce of self control within my body, I turned back around moving away from him.

I wanted to yell at him and tell him how stupid he had been. How he should have come with me. Instead, I kept on. Out on my own, I tried to sleep during the day in any brush and coverage I could find. If luck was in my favor, I'd hide out in a gas station, a store, or a restaurant where I could either get someone to let me in or break in myself.

I discovered that people were hiding from the terrorists everywhere. I also discovered evidence of what happened to those who weren't hiding. What Trey and I saw happen to people who approached them was evidently the courtesy that was given everywhere. Even though it was hard traveling in the frigid cold, it occurred to me how much worse it would be in the baking heat of summer with bodies decaying throughout the streets.

With no GPS, I needed to follow the highway to keep on route. Staying near the road was nerve-wracking, though, because by nature it had less tree and bush coverage.

Unseen, I was gaining distance and making slow progress with each passing night. Maybe my overconfidence made me sloppy. One morning, I stayed on foot too long into the dawning of daylight. Moving at a brisk pace, unwrapping a granola bar I had in my bag for breakfast, I didn't notice two foot patrol fighters approaching on the oncoming highway lanes.

They were distracted by something to their right. It appeared to be an abandoned, parked car in the grassy bank off to the side of the highway. I would have overlooked the car as simply abandoned, but the two men were suspicious of some activity and veered from the road to investigate. Their curiosity with the car was the only reason they didn't discover and execute me.

Watching with a desperate hope they would not return and find my hiding location, I remained as still as possible. If they suspected an abandoned car with such curiosity, they would surely be able to find me.

The men circled the car in opposite directions, one of them bending down to look beneath it for someone hiding there. From my point of view, peering from behind a giant concrete column structure under the overpass, it was looking like the car would not be a concern. I braced myself for their possible return. Then, I saw the guy who remained on guard while the other searched beneath the car raise his eyebrow and nod his head down at the other and then toward the trunk. In response, they both nodded in agreement. He aimed his gun at the latch of the trunk and released a damaging bullet, opening the lid.

Inside they found someone. I couldn't see from my angle who was in there but emerging with screams was a young mother holding tightly to her daughter. The little girl clung to her mom, burying her face into her chest.

"Please!" the woman begged. "Don't hurt us. We won't cause any trouble. She is just a little girl. Please!" Biting my lip in anticipation, my mouth filled with the taste of iron as blood leaked beneath my teeth. The men smirked at her pleads before they filled both mother and daughter with bullets.

It happened so fast, I couldn't contain the gasp that left my body. Not for the first time, I found myself covering my mouth so I could physically contain the sounds and responses to the horror in my viewpoint. They carried on their surveillance not on the highway, but instead over a grassy knoll.

The murder of those people was my saving grace, and I did not waste their senseless deaths by getting caught. The concrete columns became my sanctuary. I prayed they wouldn't see me as they traveled by in the opposite lane.

If I escaped this brush with death, how could I be given another free pass? My eyes closed. I swore to God I would be more careful and stay alert if I got out of this. If I was going to live, I would have to be smarter. At nightfall, I carried the heaviness of Trey, the mom, the little girl, and my salvation. I needed something to take the edge off of my pain. The breaking sadness of grief was taking hold inside of me.

Like an answered prayer, my path led me to what would be my last refuge stop. I was taken in by a middle-aged woman named Jade. She lived in a small, red farmhouse, the only color standing out in the bleak backdrop of winter. The farm sat into an enormous amount of acreage covered with tree stands which I later learned served as the boundary line to Pennsylvania.

My arrival at her modest home was early the following morning, just as the sun was starting to shine. A light was on in the back room so I could see through her front windows. It gave me pause, standing at the bottom of her sprawling porch. No one had left a light on to advertise *"we're home"* since the terror had started.

Partly, I knocked on the door to warn whoever lived here to turn the light off, but mostly I needed shelter for the day. Unexpectedly, Jade answered her door without reluctance. She didn't appear to be the least bit concerned with my impromptu visit.

She wore casual jeans and a sweatshirt that sported a middle school football team logo. Her graying, caramel hair was tied back into a low ponytail. She had thick bangs neatly sitting above her brow line and green eyes she must have been named for. Jade gave the impression she could handle herself. Maybe that's why she wasn't intimidated by my surprise visit—but dang, I really thought she ought to be.

"Hi there. I saw your light on," I reported awkwardly and pointed toward the room in the back. "I don't think that's a good idea. Ya know? They might see it and get interested in who's here." I gestured my hand behind me. "Maybe you should keep your lights off."

She smiled at me. "Oh, honey, that's real sweet of you. But they ain't botherin' me out here."

I was confused by her self-assured safety. Had she not seen any of the terror I had? Looking around her place, it did seem awfully quiet. "Are you saying they haven't been out here? Do you know what they are doing to people further into the city and suburbs?" I asked, incredulous.

"I only saw them movin' through on the highway, but I can imagine they are not invited company." She spoke to me soothingly, handing out empathy like a crisis nurse. "I have welcomed in more than a few people tryin' to flee, so I've heard a fair share of horror stories that make my blood curdle.

I'm apparently in a safe zone, because my farm sits up against the border to Pennsylvania back there." She gestured toward her yard. "There are only acres of forest between my land and the next state. From what I understand, the United States military is already heavily guardin' the borderline. In fact, they have made regular visits here to me. I've given them refugees and they've given me protection." She finished speaking and watched my reaction to her glorious news.

"Are you telling me that you are operating as a refugee camp?" I had really seen it all now. It finally sunk in my brain our country was fighting a war on our soil. I learned about this in school, saw it on the news happening to other countries, but grew up with a false narrative that it could never happen here, where I lived.

Jade nodded and extended her arm at her side as if to welcome me in. With a relieved and grateful heart, I vigorously shook my head.

We sat at her round, oak kitchen table in mismatched chairs while Jade listened to my story of trying to get back to Maryland to see Taden, including all of the hell that I had witnessed but narrowly escaped.

I focused on a vase of fake sunflowers sitting in front of me, an unsuccessful attempt to not get upset reliving the devastating events so fresh in my mind. Jade's facial expressions revealed the range of sensitivity she felt for my experiences which was making it hard for me to hold it together.

In response to a long pause I took when I got to the part about seeing the soldiers shoot down the first man that approached them, she rose up from the table and walked across the barn-board kitchen floor, which creaked when she stopped. Jade reached up into the country blue cupboards above the refrigerator and pulled out a bottle of cheap whiskey. Then she walked over to a further cupboard to get out two small glasses. After pouring a shot in each glass, she set one on the table in front of me.

"Honey, sip this slow and try to relax. It will do some good. It always does."

She sat back in her seat diagonal from me and did the same with hers. I stared hard at the whiskey. My inner recovering addict reminded me not to allow it in my body, but the devastated little girl inside told me to listen to Jade's instructions.

The smell reminded me of when I'd get a bad cold and my mom would make me a Hot Toddy. I really hated that stuff and would plead to her that it was awful, but she would tell me to drink it anyway because the strength in the drink would defeat whatever war the germs were waging on my immune system.

Sipping the whiskey like Jade had advised, I could feel the warmth and calming trickle to my nerve endings and heat up my belly.

"Our soldiers will be around, but it might be a few days. Sweetheart, you're welcome to stay on until they come through. Lord knows I could use the company. It does get somethin' lonely round here. Do you have any identification on you to show them who you are? They usually ask for that when they arrive."

I nodded that I did have I.D. In fact, I still had my personal item bag from the flight, which I fumbled around in to locate my documents. It was a gift from Taden this past Christmas, and I had wanted her to see that I was using it. This brown, leather bag was the only accessory I owned without some type of flash. It certainly was a Taden thing to go neutral on a style choice. I felt pretty thankful that I had used it. Being a backpack type of purse, it made keeping my belongings and food easier while constantly on the move. My mind wandered to Jade.

"How come you don't leave? You have the chance to get out and start fresh without living each day with danger lurking outside your door. So, why do you stay?"

She pulled in a deep and thoughtful breath of air, shrugged her shoulders, and then let her head fall back so that her eyes fixed onto the ceiling. She looked like she was trying to pick the best starting spot for her answer.

"I've considered that maybe leavin' my farm would be better for me than stayin', but then I think about my husband and my boy. They are there, you know." She tilted her head toward me and lifted her glass in my direction to emphasize this blowing news. "They went into the city for the weekend to catch a game. It was the same weekend the tanks rolled in. I haven't seen or heard from either of 'em since. I *can't* leave here if they are still out there tryin' to get back to me. I have to hold onto hope that there is someone given 'em refuge." She nodded her head like she was convincing herself it was true. "If I stay here and keep other people safe, maybe the universe will return the favor to me and keep my boys safe." Her eyes welled up with tears, and I couldn't stop myself from going over to hug and comfort her. She laughed through her pain, patting my hand on her shoulder and added, "I've always hated football! I blame it all on football!"

The resistance soldiers Jade spoke of did not come for several weeks. Throughout that time, I helped out around the house and passed the days hanging out with her. My mind wandered to the cupboard above her fridge every single day since the whiskey had blissfully numbed my pain. In an effort to distract from the urge to drink more, we played so many board games I think I'll be gamed out for the rest of my life. While we couldn't get any reception on the television, Jade had an archaic VCR player hooked up to an equally ancient TV in her basement, along with a plastic tub full of VHS tapes that were hers when she was a kid. It was insanely entertaining to hunker down and watch old movies with Jade in an effort to deal with my world of emotional stress.

It was the start of twilight when Jade's soldiers finally came to her front door. She welcomed them in and prepared a meal. We sat in her dining room and she explained to them how I came to be her temporary roommate.

Rather quickly, it was my turn to tell the stories which had already become difficult for me to believe had ever really happened. In the midst of recounting details from my escape, I could feel my core body temperature drop and a shiver take hold of me. Jade noticed and pulled a crochet blanket off the back of her couch in the next room to lay over my shoulders. It was like my body was palpably preparing to deal with facing the part of my story that included Trey and the stark sound of the pop I believed came from his gun *and* the promise I made to him that I would not turn back. I reported the deaths of the mother and daughter hiding in the trunk of the car just before I arrived here. They listened to every word I uttered without a single interruption.

After examining my license and passport, they finally agreed to escort me to Pennsylvania which, they explained, had not been infiltrated by The Reckoners (what they called the terrorists). I felt irritated that I had wasted so much time waiting for these people to arrive when I could've left on my own. They had made it sound like the travel from Jade's to the border wasn't dangerous at all. I had so many questions I wanted to ask but it seemed so did they. It was mutually agreed that once we crossed the border, we could entertain both sides of the question and answer sequence.

I couldn't thank Jade enough for what she had done for me. She deserved more. Her husband. Her son. I couldn't help but think she was right about the universe. It had to be taking care of her guys. I left with the hope I would see Jade again to properly thank her, and that she would be with her family the next time I did. The trip from Jade's farm to Pennsylvania took about an hour, but I was finally out of New York and for the first time since I left the airport, I felt safe. Until, they detained me.

It did seem a little bit too easy.

I lost track of how long I was held in detainment. They kept me in a tiny, windowless room with fluorescent lighting, connected to a bathroom big enough to hold a toilet and standing shower. The room looked like it used to be an office, and was furnished with a couch, a shelf of books, and a little kitchenette.

I spent most of my time reading the random collection of books that I found on the shelf. Each day, a minimum of three different intelligence officers would send for me to discuss the details of my escape from New York. I told them all I could but it was never enough. They believed that I was withholding details or lying to them. I was becoming desperate.

"Listen! I don't know what else you want from me! I've told you everything I know. I have cooperated with you, but you haven't answered any of my questions. Please at least tell me if these people have attacked Maryland!"

I got the impression they were deciding whether or not I might be a spy for The Reckoning. Even if they had believed I wasn't a spy, they weren't letting me go until they were sure I'd reported every single event I witnessed in excruciating detail. Which I had. Reliving every aspect of my experiences over and over again was not boding well in my psyche. I was becoming hopeless and depressed.

As the days mounted nothing improved and it didn't feel like an end was in sight. I decidedly became less and less cooperative. When I did speak to the officers, it was only to persist in getting to Taden.

Finally, in an attempt to appease me so I would cooperate and tell them what they thought I knew but was withholding, they entertained the idea of bringing in my sister. In the process of verification to locate Taden, they discovered that my sister was Dr. Taden Barrett of the NIST. After that, it was only a few hours until our old neighbor, Dr. Pasterski appeared.

Although I was not anticipating seeing her, I didn't find it unbelievable. She had always been sort of like a fairy godmother to us. Especially Taden. Dr. Pasterski was the reason that Taden became a physicist, and, here she was to take care of me like the old days.

She walked through the door with an air of importance and dignity that demanded respect. Her confidence bathed me in calmness and I took a deep, grateful breath that she was here with me.

"Ruth! My dear, you're safe now. All the necessary documents have been completed. We can leave and go see your sister. I'm sure you can't wait to get out of here." At the mention of Taden, my head fell into my hands and I crumbled forward in the chair I sat on until my body was being supported by the desk I had repeatedly been interrogated at. "Aw, honey! It's okay. I'm here now," she said as she rubbed my back.

It was reassuring to have Dr. Pasterski mothering me in the way I always found myself needing. I tried to stop my burning eyes and quivering chin from making a scene. She put her arm around my shoulders and guided me out the door like I was a little girl again.

I hadn't seen Taden since she visited me at Christmas. Throughout this entire ordeal, I couldn't help but replay every conversation we had that holiday break as if they were the last we would ever have. I didn't know if she was dead or alive. I had no idea if she was safe or not. It was excruciating to wonder about her all this time. Since the official news from Dr. Pasterski that she was both alive and safe, I could not stand to be away from her another day.

Unfortunately, we had to drive the rest of the way through Pennsylvania and into Maryland until we got home to Gaitherberg. I was so exhausted from the emotional drainage of my detainment that I drifted in and out of wakeful sleep throughout the drive. Dr. Pasterski sat in the back of the vehicle with her arm around me while her associate drove.

My mind acted as a personal playlist of memories with Taden. The memory my mind replayed the longest was the day Taden was off to college.

 Taden had on the University of Pennsylvania sweatshirt I got her as a congratulations gift for starting her freshman year. I was bursting with pride at the sight of her in it.

After a long week of packing, her moving boxes were loaded in the U-Haul we rented, ready for the drive to Pennsylvania.

While Taden was over at Dr. Pasterski's saying goodbye, I had been busy all morning packing up the kitchen. It was the last unpacked room left in the apartment. I didn't want to stay there even one night alone, so my plan was to leave for L.A. from an airport in Pennsylvania after I got Taden to school and helped her settle into her dorm. Dr. Pasterski offered to arrange for the movers to bring my things to California, then donate the rest. Taden and I agreed to say goodbye to our home one last time that afternoon.

I looked up from the box I had been filling with utensils to see Taden had returned from Dr. Pasterski's and was tearfully watching me from the living room. She was standing exactly where our Mom's bed was parked the last few months of her life. Her arms were folded around herself, as if she squeezed tightly enough she could hold in the emotions she was on the verge of letting out.

I closed the box and taped it up, then walked over to her, knowing this was the last time our lives would be like this, together, *family*. "Are you ready Taden?" She knew I didn't mean "ready to go." I was making sure she was ready for goodbye.

She didn't answer my question, but instead dove into me with a desperation I could easily match.

Together, we walked out the front door one final time. Taden closed and locked it behind us. I put my hand on the door to physically let the place go. The long seconds dragged into short minutes standing still. Taden finally took my hand and pulled me forward. I sighed because while most of the days in that home felt like they aged me exponentially, the years of us together, in that home, were much too quick. One foot in front of the other, neither of us turning back, we moved onto the next place.

CHAPTER 11

By late afternoon we had finally arrived at the NIST building. It was the first time I had ever been to Taden's office. Even though I was used to being surrounded by tall buildings in Los Angeles, back home it wasn't so common and I caught myself reacting to the sheer presence of the building. It was quite impressive and mildly intimidating. Which of the thousands of windows belonged to my smarty-pants sister?

Without Dr. Pasterski, I wouldn't have gotten inside the building. Security was tight as a result of the terrorists. I hadn't known that Taden's job was of such priority to the government. To be honest, I didn't totally get what she actually *did*. I've always known she was smart—like, beyond smart. I didn't even really know what physics was. As crazy science smart as I believed Taden to be, it might not have totally sunk in the level of her genius until I was walking in her world.

The further we traveled into the building, the heavier my chest felt. Tingling in my fingertips alerted me to breathe as I looked down and noticed purple take hold of my hands. I was wrought with anticipation to see Taden safe again.

Dr. Pasterski paused outside of two swinging glass doors to swipe her badge, granting us clearance into my sister's laboratory. Before we went in, she looked at me sweetly.

"We're here, my girl. Are you ready? She's going to be so happy to see you!" Dr. Pasterski led the way into the bright white laboratory.

My eyes searched maniacally among the people buzzing around the room. There was a mixture of camouflaged soldiers, business people in important looking suits, and scientists in white lab coats. Across the room, I spotted her among the science group. No longer able to contain myself, I called out her name and ran to her with my arms open.

Startled by my commotion she (along with every other person in the room) looked up from what she was doing. Through my tear-blurred vision I recognized her response upon registering my face.

With complete disregard for her surroundings, Taden crumpled to the ground, like she commonly did as a kid if her emotions were too heavy for her to hold onto.

My arms wrapped around her and we stayed there in the middle of all of the white coats and camo. Several of our onlookers joined in our crying caucus, including some tough-looking soldiers.

That made one man in particular stand out when he gave the impression we were wasting his time. He looked familiar, and I thought maybe I had seen that guy in my sister's pictures online. Was that Marius? Whoever he was, he gave me the impression we should get up and move our reunion to a more private location.

In Taden's office, we sat huddled together on the floor until we were caught up with each other. I told her every detail that had happened since the day Maria asked me to visit Maryland. We both agreed somehow Maria must have known about The Reckoning before it happened. Overcome with worry about Maria, I began to cry.

"Taden, If she knew stuff, she's probably not safe right now. Why didn't she come with me?"

Taden had met Maria a few times from the visits she made out to L.A. They got along really well, leaving me feeling warm and fuzzy inside. Taden was typically a good judge of character, almost too careful about selecting the people in her life. The fact that they clicked led me to trust Maria even more than I already did.

It was obvious Taden was trying to distract me from worrying with the delivery of her news bomb. "Ruth, I have a huge secret. I don't know what to do though. I want to tell you. I NEED to tell you. But it's national security. I'm sworn to keep silent, like under oath."

"That's ridiculous! This is not the time for secrets. Besides, I think the country has more important fish to fry."

Before Taden spilled the details, she made me promise not to tell anyone and I had to show her I understood that her job and the country depended on it. Even for a scientist, she could be pretty dramatic when it came to following the rules.

"I'm trusting you with the biggest secret of all time."

My eyes widened getting irritated with how long and drawn out she was making this admission. "I've got it. Either tell me or don't."

You know how I've always been fascinated with time travel?" I nodded. "About a year ago, I figured it out."

My face screwed up into a confusion. "Huh? What are you talking about?"

"I cracked the code. It started with an object and then we worked up to simple life forms until I started going back in time myself."

I blinked rapidly while she spoke. I didn't quite grasp what she was telling me. I heard the words but the sense of it wasn't sinking into my brain. "Are you telling me you can go back in time?"

"Yes. That is exactly what I am telling you. I've gone back a few times. We're about to go on a military mission to fifteen years ago. To stop all of this."

As she unfolded her discoveries of time travel, I couldn't help but feel like I was being told a fictional story. Then she explained to me what The Reckoning was about and why time travel was needed to end it. I was sort of losing my grip on reality. It was hard enough to accept that our country was fighting a war on our land, but then to add this other piece of time travel to the puzzle was just too much to take in.

Taden validated my overwhelming senses. "Believe me, I get how you're feeling. I was shocked when I had to process The Reckoning for the first time and know you were in the thick of it. Plus, I know on top of everything else you have to be freaking out about the time travel part."

Once Taden got the major storylines out of her system, we sat in silence. I laid my head on her shoulder trying to be present in the moment digesting all of the information she had delivered. A half hour passed easily while we settled into the quiet, appreciating that we were together. The trance was broken with a gentle tap on the door, followed by Dakotah poking her head in.

"Are you two okay in here?" She looked about the room to find where we were. Taden shot her hand up in the air.

"We're back here. We're good. Just catching up. Thanks."

"Can I get either of you anything?"

I responded with a request for whiskey to which Taden gave me a disapproving look. "What? I was kidding. It's a lot to take in. Just a joke."

"Alright. Let me know if you change your mind or need anything. I wanted to check in and make sure everything was alright."

After she left, I sat upright and turned my body towards my sister. "Okay. Time travel. Got it. Sort of. You want to get back out there and introduce me to your time travel friends?"

"Well, you just met Dakotah. She's on my team. She's a really good friend too. You still have to meet Abel and Marius."

"Oh yeah, Marius! It is time, sister of mine," rubbing my hands together like meeting her boyfriend was the most important event of this insane day that I learned my sister was a time travel scientist.

In a nervous, schoolgirl way, she ushered me through the hallway back to the lab, and from around the corner she pointed him out to me, trying to squash her beaming smile. Whispering, so no one would hear her acting so giddy, "He's right there, talking to Dr. Pasterski. Isn't he hot?"

"Yep. He's a hottie." I tried to cover my disappointment at confirming the too-cool-to-show-emotion guy was indeed the one from Taden's pictures. "I have more to tell you."

With a deep inhale, not sure how much more I could handle, I looked at her expectantly. "Not here. I can't tell you here." Her goofy smile led us back to her office where we resumed Taden's full disclosure.

Settling back into our hiding spots on the floor behind her desk, she lowered her voice again. "Marius has a plan for the two of us to travel back in time to the week that mom died. He doesn't want me to tell the rest of the team or our bosses. He thinks we should go back together in secret. I desperately want to go with him but as a scientist I feel obliged to uphold a moral code not to use this technology for personal gain." As she finished, her eyes implored me to tell her what she wanted to hear.

Only a guy that smooth would tempt Taden to break protocol. She was the most rule-following person I had ever known. Not only was he suggesting she break the rules, but he wanted her to use this discovery for personal reasons and lie to everyone who trusted her.

But couldn't she see that life experience led her to who she is now? I knew she felt responsible for my drug habit and, even though she didn't say so, preventing me from starting must have been part of her agenda going back.

But I felt my battle with addiction made me a stronger person, and I wasn't sure I'd be as successful as I was without having to overcome the adversity it brought into my life.

I tried to speak to her rule-following conscience. "Taden, this has to break some type of code of ethics."

I could tell when Taden was hearing my words but choosing not to accept them. This wasn't what she was hoping to get from me. Diverting her eyes from mine, she looked down at the floor. I was not Taden's mother, and we had both been taking care of ourselves for quite some time. Toning it down a little, I shared my thoughts with her honestly.

"Listen. What you choose to do is your choice and I won't fight you on it."

Fear of what could come of this crept into my awareness. I felt a minute level of comfort that she had confided in me about Marius's plan, and if she was gone with him to our past at least I would know about it.

Taden recognized the worrying I was engaged in. "We will only be gone for a day. We won't stay long. Just long enough to see mom. Say what I need to say and come home. To you it won't even feel like we've gone. We will come back to the very moment we left. No one will be the wiser. Marius looks out for me and keeps me safe. He won't let anything happen to me. You don't need to worry."

From the way she was trying to convince me it was okay, I concluded that she had already decided she was going. Her only problem was that she still doubted it was the right choice to make. It was deeply concerning how this man was able to pull her off track. I had never seen anyone who was able to get Taden off track.

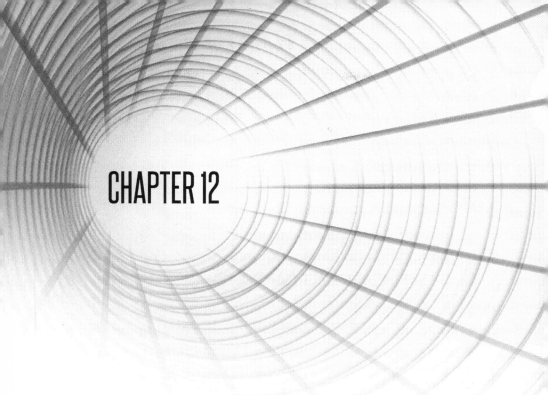

CHAPTER 12

The night Taden and Marius left, she hugged me goodbye longer than a normal Taden hug would last, which made me worry that she was saying a real goodbye and not, "see you later." I shrugged it off, because if nothing else it had become clear to me over the past few days that my sister was about as badass of a scientist as anyone could be. She knew what she was doing.

That was a long day. I expected she would come home after work like normal.

She convinced me nothing would seem different since the two of them would return to the moment they time traveled from. Nonetheless, I went through the motions of the day while running scenarios through my mind of all that could go wrong. I tried to fill my time with busywork. I cleaned up Taden and Marius's apartment, which looked like they hadn't done in months. Funny enough, it didn't feel like that long ago cleaning up after Taden was my life's story. She may have been an intellectual, but she seriously neglected her living conditions.

No matter how I stayed busy or attempted to keep my mind off of the insane realities facing me, I could not stop thinking about the whiskey Jade gave me and how badly I needed it. Desperate to distract my thoughts of Taden, whiskey, and what was happening to Maria in L.A., I tried to read a book from my sister's library. The stir-crazy feeling exploded when Taden's promise she would be back after work did not hold up.

I tried not to panic, but rather quickly I found myself at the NIST building. In my haste, I'd forgotten the level of security at the lab and had to locate Dr. Pasterski to vouch for me. By the time I was relaying where Taden was and that she hadn't come back, I had worked myself into a tizzy and had effectively gotten Dr. Pasterski and Taden's friends, Dakotah and Abel, into a panic along with me. I was supposed to keep this a secret between me and my sister, but her safety took priority. For all I knew, this Marius guy was way more trouble than I had anticipated.

Almost as soon as I revealed to them where Taden was, they were outraged. Both Dakotah and Abel directed their anger solely at Marius. Neither of them trusted him with Taden. Back and forth, they recounted several incidents of strange behavior from him over the past couple months. They settled in agreement that there was enough justification to fear for her safety and go after her. Dr. Pasterski was too astounded from learning Taden had time jumped with Marius to really participate in the character attacks on him.

Abel, who was quickly getting things ready to travel back to find Taden, purposefully inquired, "Ruth, can you tell us the exact time I should be traveling to? We will need to know the year, month and day to calculate the distance backward I will have to go. I will also need to know the exact location." I followed him around with my arms dangling at my sides, feeling helpless. I needed to go too. *How could I just stand here and wait?*

Meanwhile, Dakotah was busy pounding away on the keyboard at her computer station, followed by frantically getting some type of injection ready for Abel. After I told them when in time to travel to, I made an appeal for Abel to take me with him.

"I can make this go so much faster! I know exactly where to go if she is trying to get to our mom before she dies. Plus, I know all the spots Taden would be in if she's not at home. You *need* me!"

It was true. If they didn't want to leave Taden in the past with Marius any longer than possible, Abel was going to need someone who knew our old stomping grounds.

He concurred that I might be an asset on this trip. However, he wasn't exactly excited at the prospect of a travel companion. He closed his eyes tightly and shook his head demonstrating how reluctantly he agreed to take me along.

Before I could really grasp that I would be traveling in time, Dakotah was rolling up my sleeve and strapping a really tight band on my arm, ready to inject me with a serum that would forever change my future.

 I enjoy stories. I love reading books, watching TV shows, and movies. I've always thought everything would be simpler if we could just dissolve from one scene to the next, the way it's done in stories. Life would be *so* much easier.

Time travel felt *just* like that. One minute I was flipping out about Taden, in the next, boom! I dissolved. New scene: *my past*. It felt like I came undone and then redone in the same amount of time it takes to turn a light switch. It also sort of felt like being high.

It was like a strange dream, arriving at our old apartment building. Climbing the stairs to our floor was so familiar it seemed like I had just done this hike yesterday. I practically floated to our entryway, then lifted up on my tiptoes to peek into the small windows on our front door. Peering in, I saw *myself*. There sat 18-year-old me, folding laundry on the living room couch. I was reeling from the time jump, but this sight was a feeling which cannot be put into words: to see my past self living a day I remembered living.

Looking beyond myself, I could see my mom on her bed, which we had moved into our living room. The two of us were watching *Gilmore Girls,* as would be expected. The initial sight of us there in all that pain (my mom's mostly physical and mine emotional) stopped my breath. I had buried my feelings of utter tragedy deep inside of me so that not a thing on the planet could unearth them. Except, it seemed, the moments that created my pain in the first place.

Abel put his hand on my shoulder. "You okay?" he asked. "What do you see?"

"I can see me and…and my mom in the living room, but Taden doesn't seem to be home. You know, teenage Taden. What should we do now?"

"We should knock on the door and see what we can find out. Are you going to be okay talking to this version of yourself?" He gestured with his head toward the door. He looked concerned that I might not be able to handle it, and suggested, "If it's too much, you could wait around the corner and let me do the talking."

I assured him I would be fine. "There is no way 18-year-old Ruth would open up the door to some strange man alone on the other side. She is too careful for that. If we want her to answer, I better do the knocking." He laughed and pulled a picture of Marius out of his pocket. I knocked on the door, and within seconds was face to face with myself.

It was bizarre, but wasn't exactly like staring into a mirror. Younger Ruth ironically struck me as much older. She was dressed like a new mom without any time for self care. Her hair was haphazardly pulled back into a messy bun that appeared days old, she had bags under her eyes that told on her sleepless nights, and her face held the look one gets when being pulled in too many directions. I was sure that young Ruth would never suspect she was talking to her future self. Standing in front of her, my appearance suggested I was even younger than she was. Plus, *I knew* I was talking to myself and *still* had a difficult time believing it.

There were so many things I wanted to tell her. Girl, go out with your friends. Say yes to that person who has been trying to date you at school. Get out of those scrubby clothes and show off that rockin' teenage body. Don't take those pills. Whatever you do, *stop* hiding out in this apartment.

Processing all these thoughts demanded my full attention. Abel would have to do the talking after all. I encountered a wormhole that left me entranced.

"Hi there, I'm Abel and this is…" he paused, not sure how to introduce me.

His voice invited me to rejoin reality. They were both looking at me, waiting for me to speak.

"Hello, I'm Maria." She was the only name on the tip of my tongue. "My friend and I were hoping you could help us find someone."

She politely smiled at us and took a quick glance over her shoulder to check that Mom was doing alright. It was a nearly undetectable gesture, one I almost forgot being a part of my daily life. I fought the urge to reach out to myself and offer her a comforting hug. I knew how much I was craving someone to hug me like they were going to take care of me.

Again, I was snapped back into the current moment by Abel. He showed Ruth Marius's picture. "Have you by chance seen this man?"

The look on her face told us she had. "Oh! Yes," she replied. "I had the strangest encounter with him the other day. Come on in for a minute." She welcomed us in the foyer just outside our living room.

I was literally ten steps away from Mom. Even though I wanted to soak in the sight of her, I kept my eyes on Ruth as she continued talking. "It started with a phone call from my mom's new doctor. He told me she had an appointment at their facility in town for a few tests but had not showed up. I was surprised because I'm usually good at keeping track of my mom's doctor appointments, but I guess it can get excessive at times and I miss some things, so I didn't question it. I hustled to get my mom in the car. Thankfully, they didn't cancel it. When I arrived, that man in your picture greeted us." She pointed at Marius in the photo Abel pinched between his fingers.

"What specifically did he want to help your mom with?" I asked her, bewildered.

Ruth had no good explanation. "I don't know. It was really weird. He asked a few questions, briefly looked at my mom, then abruptly told us he couldn't help us. I was disappointed and shocked at how absurd the whole visit felt. I wanted to complain to someone on the way out, but my mom was exhausted from the entire ordeal and I just wanted to get her home. I totally disliked that guy. He was a real jerk."

We agreed with Ruth's summation of Marius. Abel still needed more information, so he pressed further. "Can you tell us where this office is located?"

Ruth explained where to go and described the hospital to be an unmarked building on the outside. The inside looked like a normal hospital, only with hardly any patients in it. She started biting her cuticles. "Should I be scared? Are we in some kind of danger?"

I knew exactly how her mind worked, of course, and I knew she was already concocting some terrible version of this story in her head. I also knew that in her wildest imagination, she could never come up with the awful reality about Marius.

Ruth had already lost almost every important person in her life at a young age. Her youth had been snatched away and replaced with grief, responsibility, and loneliness. I wished I could remove these events. It would save me a lot of sleepless nights, and push me onto a path of happiness much more quickly.

However, I thought that maybe this was how it should happen. Maybe a person is only ready to become who they are meant to be at the right moment of time. Maybe that time doesn't come until after difficult experiences. I might have cheated myself out of important self growth if I tried to solve all of Ruth's hardships back in time.

What I found most strange as I stayed up in my brain was that I had a memory of being here. I remembered the day that I took Mom to that weird doctor's appointment that young Ruth described. I remembered before she even finished describing it, and I remembered answering the door to Abel, with his picture of Marius, and Maria. I thought Maria was beautiful. I imagined how her life must be and how I wished I could live like her. All that time, it was *me* that I wanted to become. It was incredible to remember how I looked at my older self back then. Teenage Ruth could see how comfortable I was in my own skin, and how proud of my body I had learned to become. I was my own role model. It was from this meeting with myself that sparked the inward changes I would be making in the years to come. I wanted to be just like "Maria."

In the back of my mind, I was conscious of the fact that we had to get out of there. Ruth finished explaining to Abel where the hospital was, and if he didn't nudge me to leave, I probably would've stood there staring at myself all day, regardless of my common sense telling me to go.

Before leaving, I responded to her question of fear about Marius. "Ruth, you don't have anything to worry about. We've been trying to locate this doctor for awhile. We just have some questions to ask him. You did everything right. I know this might sound strange coming from a person you don't know, but I think you are a pretty awesome young woman. You are taking care of things around here like a boss. I'm really impressed. Thanks for answering our questions. It was great to meet you."I motioned for Abel to join me on the way out.

A few steps toward the door, I stopped and whipped around to my mom lying on her deathbed. Ruth widened her eyes at me. She was re-thinking whether or not she should be worried about me. I said an extra goodbye to my mom telepathically, and at that exact instant, she half opened her eyes, reached out her hand, and called for Ruth. I knew she was calling for *me*. She could feel *me* there, she was a part of me, and was still deeply connected to me no matter what timeline I was from. My very DNA ran through her before it was mine. She loved me, cared for me, knew me, and celebrated me. She was *exactly* who and what I had missed so terribly all these years. She was my mom. My mom stood at the gates to leave this world, but still she reached out for *me*.

Ruth ran to her as she said goodbye to us over her shoulder. I wiped my eyes and walked out the front door again. This time it was much harder to leave.

Late that afternoon, we arrived at the unmarked building Ruth sent us to. Abel directed me how we would get in and find Taden. I was vaguely familiar with the place, after having recalled being here with Mom.

Once inside, we first disguised ourselves with hospital scrubs found in a supply closet and then located the security monitors. The security station was oddly unmanned. Abel searched through the building's various cameras. Mostly the monitors revealed a pretty regular looking hospital, until he flipped past a channel that reminded me of an evil scientist's lab. It wasn't as big as Taden's lab at the NIST, but it certainly looked like a place that some mad brainiacs could spend their time. Abel kept flipping through until we found the camera in Taden's room.

I couldn't believe what I was seeing. My sister was tied to a bed like she was going to hurt someone. *I* wanted to hurt someone. I would have loved to have come face to face with Marius at that moment. Abel led the way to her floor.

It felt absurd that I was following around a time travel scientist/government soldier in a fake hospital tracking down my genius, hostage sister. Then again, I just had a conversation with my teenage self and said goodbye to my mom again after jumping backward in time. My brain was swimming in disbelief, wrapped carefully with absolute belief.

Once inside her room, I felt even more sick at the sight of Taden tied down to a bed. She was clearly distraught, visible signs of emotional torture written across her face. "Oh my God, Taden!" I uttered, one hand covering my mouth, the other grasping my heart in disbelief.

Abel was already busy disconnecting her monitors. I found myself petting her hair in distress. I used to smooth her hair when she was distraught as a kid. It calmed me as much as it did her. I ran my hands over her auburn hair again and again.

As soon as her monitors had all been removed, we worked together on releasing her restraints. Taden had been mumbling incoherently, but when the restraints came off, she started speaking more clearly.

Taden looked at me hard, and with an attempt of dominance in her voice she yelled, "I am not crazy! And I know it! You are *not* here. I just saw you leave with Mom, and you were a teenager. I can't possibly know what you look like as an old woman. You are not here. You are not here."

It was the cherry on top of a hard-to-swallow sundae.

She kept squeezing her eyes closed tight, then opening them to see if we had gone.

I interrupted, "Whoa, whoa! Old woman? That's a little harsh, Tay, don't you think?"

She quickly shut her eyes again and pressed them together much harder, like that would make me poof out of this God-forsaken room. Taden peeled her eyes open again, dismayed we were still there.

She looked at Abel and forced herself to announce, "I know you aren't here because I completely made you up. You don't exist. My brain designed a hero and put *your* face on it. I have to get home to my mom and they won't let me go if you are here! Please leave." Abel might have been a tough soldier type, but his Achilles heel was pretty clear; having Taden say these things to him looked to be causing him actual pain. I knew the longer we were there, the more difficult and dangerous our exit would become, so I took over from Abel's unsuccessful attempts to pull her back into reality.

After a few minutes of failed attempts to reason with my sister, I finally convinced her we were actually there by explaining how I had just left our mom's bedside. "Taden, I don't even know how to explain the bizarre feelings that rushed through my body, seeing my teenage self face to face. It was like watching an old home movie, but interactive. I will need years of therapy to break it down, but what therapist would listen to this story and not think I'm a lunatic?" I had a good laugh at my own insanity before returning to the heaviness of the moment. I leaned over my sister's face. "Taden, I need you to be okay now. You are my only family."

Taden carefully studied me while I told her my story, but it wasn't totally convincing her. Toward the end I saw a look of terror cross her face, and she put her hands over her body, feeling around at her skin. Something triggered her, and it was then that she accepted she was not a kid and all of her memories were real.

In disbelief, she stared at the bed she had just been tied to before remorsefully looking to Abel. Turning her glance to the ground, she whispered to him, "I'm sorry. I'm so sorry I doubted..." and her voice trailed off.

Because she was looking at her feet instead of at Abel she missed his reaction to her, but I didn't. I saw his relief that she believed in him again, and I saw him start toward her as if he was going to embrace her longingly, but before he could reach her she started begging us to take her back to our old neighborhood.

She flailed her body toward me. "I need to go next door and talk to Dr. Pasterski. It's important that I tell her about Marius. He is not who he says he is. Who knows what he's going to do! He could even be a part of the craziness going on back home. If it's even possible, we need to let her know."

She realized I wasn't making the decisions about our safety and where we were headed to next, so she traded her pleading to Abel, who was peering out the door he had slightly cracked open.

"Abel! Close the door. Look at me." He did so, like an obedient student. "I know your priority is to get us out of here. I understand. But if we can get to Dr. Pasterski and tell her about Marius, maybe it could help. Whatever happens to us right now, it's worth the risk," she finished, with a pointed assurance in her plan.

Abel appeared torn. He gazed into Taden's eyes for a few slow seconds like a key trying to unlock a door. The trouble was he got stuck there before finally getting it to open.

"Okay Taden, you have a point," he said, then smiled mischievously. "And as my boss, I am compelled to follow your orders here." Then he became much more serious again, the tone of his voice like a stern father. "However, you need to realize the danger you are in." He stepped toward Taden and grasped her arms. "Marius will discover you are gone, and once he realizes I am here to bring you back he will be coming for us. Not to mention we don't know if he's working with others." Hesitantly, he let go of her arms and took a step back. "You are a treasure to national security, and I have sworn my life to protect you and return you to safety. Do you understand what that means Taden?"

CHAPTER 13

TADEN

"I understand." I was stunned by the way Abel had just looked at me. I couldn't recall ever looking into his eyes for that long. There was a connection I felt, and I didn't quite understand it. He conveyed layers of emotions without saying a word. Certain he was attempting to communicate something without words, our connection broke the instant he took his hands from me and looked away. I wished he would just tell me what he wanted me to know. We didn't have time for a secret unspoken language.

I was a matter of national security. He was just doing his job.

"We need to get going! Right?" I asked him, in order to leave this painful, self-indulgent moment behind. In response, he scooped me into his arms and carried me out. It felt like I had been waiting for him to do that forever.

The late afternoon sun had finally let go of the day, allowing for evening dusk to ascend with our arrival at Dr. Pasterski's house. I was acutely aware that my mom was right next door. At the other end of the path beyond the glowing street lamps between her house and our apartment lay closure I never got to have.

Her brightly-lit porch revealed a partially open front door. Abel took the lead and pulled out his gun. He put his finger to his mouth to signal to us to be silent. I grabbed hold of Ruth's hand and she pulled me close to her.

We quietly stalked through her enormous house, taking in the sights of forced entry. Everything was turned around and strewn all over. Tables were on their sides. Drawers were left open. There was no sign of Dr. Pasterski, and I was beginning to fear the worst. The fact that we had time traveled here could alter the outcome of events. It wasn't clear what Marius was up to or why but finding her house broken into and he being the only time traveler not present left me to suspect this was his work. With so much unknown about Marius I didn't feel confident that he wouldn't harm Dr. Pasterski if he felt obliged. His actions could alter our timeline so that Dr. Pasterski might not survive this night and in turn cease to exist in the future. Part of why I felt compelled to travel in these first missions was so that I could collect data about the rules and guidelines of how the technology worked. It was a learning curve and the outcomes were building my data set.

Ever so quietly, we crept down the wide hallway leading to her laboratory and paused to listen for any evidence that the intruder was lingering. A rustling sound came unexpectedly from the closet across from her lab, just feet from where we stood. My heart skipped a beat and the breath in my chest felt frozen. Abel put his hand up to warn us to stop. I had no intention of moving, anyway. He crept toward the closet door for an eternity. Once he had his hand on the handle and his gun ready to fire, he swung the door open and stood on defense.

Dr. Pasterski was huddled in the back of the closet floor, her knees to her chest and her arms holding herself in. Her face was buried into her legs and she was rocking slightly. Her eyes lifted from the fetal position to see she was not in danger.

She put her hands out to me and then to Ruth, like she knew who we were without having to be told. In our embrace on the floor, she subsided into a breakdown. I had never seen this much emotion come out of Dr. Pasterski in all the years I had known her. I didn't know she even felt emotions this strongly. It puzzled me that she seemed to recognize us and continued to add to my wonderment when she began to speak to us.

"Oh Taden, I'm so relieved you're here. Ruth! My goodness, girls, look at you. You're a picture. You've grown up so nicely. Still together, Ruth and Taden. Oh girls!"

"I'm so sorry this happened to you!" I said, "Did you see who did this?"

"Unfortunately, I did not see anyone. I feel confident it was only one person though. I was walking down the hallway when my front door busted open, and so I quickly hid in the closet. I remained here praying I would not be discovered, listening to him move through my home tearing everything apart. I think he was looking for my keys. I could hear him mumbling to himself and swearing in a rage. He was trying to force entry into my lab. I *always* keep the door locked. He was in a hurry, and not long after he realized he wasn't going to get in he gave up and left. I was too scared to come out."

I looked up at Abel, and he nodded in agreement. Marius. Abel excused himself to patrol the house.

"I am a bit surprised you recognize us. Why don't you seem shocked by us being here?"

Her response left me awestruck. "I know you traveled from the future. This is what I devoted my life to. I have this laboratory in my home, next to you, so you can discover time travel."

Enough absolutely ridiculous things had taken place that day that her revelation of always knowing I would discover time travel shouldn't have felt as flabbergasting as it did.

"Sweetheart, you told your father!" she went on. "As an adult, you visited him on a time travel to the past to share with him what you accomplished. Many years ago, when he came to me and told me this, you were such a young girl. I couldn't dare believe him right away. But, he had the most impeccable details, and you had given him basic science theories to share with me so I would eventually know this was the truth. From then on, your father spent all his free time invested in you girls. You gifted him with a clear vision that his daughters were to become great and his time with you precious. His focus with you Taden was allowing you to build and investigate as much as possible. When you were ready for me to step in and begin mentoring you in physics, a home with a laboratory was just *conveniently* right in your backyard, ready for you to explore. My dear, *you* have always been the one who laid out your destiny. If only your father could have been here to see you pull it off. In a way, I guess he was already given that gift when you visited him, all those years ago."

I was unable to speak or think clearly upon hearing Dr. Pasterski explain how I became a physicist. How I discovered time travel. It was a loop of which I could not grasp the origin. Somewhere in time, I must have figured it out. I had not yet visited my father, as Dr. Pasterski said I had. Somewhere in the future I had already gone back to him. My head was spinning.

"Dr. Pasterski, are you telling me my father worked with you? In the Patriot Party?" I let that question spill out of my mouth before my brain had consciously acknowledged the link between them.

"Your father played an important role in the start of the Patriots. He was a founding member, and the first to realize a rebel group of anarchists was plotting to break apart the United States. He was on the cusp of finding out who some of the key members were when he was killed." As she said the last part, her voice trailed off and she moved her attention to her hands she was busily wringing together. We were told a vague story of how our dad had a heart attack and died at work. There was never any suspicion on our part that wasn't the truth. I sat with my mouth gaped open.

Ruth got up from where she was sitting and walked over to Dr. Pasterski. Crouching down, she put her arms around our sweet neighbor, tears spilling out of her eyes, and pulled herself cheek to cheek with Dr. Pasterski. "You've been our guardian angel ever since. Thank you for looking out for us all of those years and getting Taden onto the path she needed."

As soon as Ruth uttered those last two words, I snapped out of my shock and saw my exit. I only had this chance to break the chains of regret from my soul. Even though I hadn't yet revealed Marius to Dr. Pasterski, I was up and running out the door before Ruth could stand back up from their embrace. Abel was guarding the front door, so I decided the quickest way out would be the back. I heard Ruth yell to stop me, but still I ran. She called for Abel, and I knew he would be steps behind me before I would even reach the building, but still I ran, and I ran even faster.

In the dark, I looked for my younger self so I could tell her to go home tonight, not to Dr. Pasterski's. I was nowhere to be found. I ran into the building and up the stairs. I heard Abel and Ruth right behind me, yelling at me to stop the whole way. They wouldn't be able to catch me at this point. Their priority was my safety, and I was fine. I opened the door, fled down the hall, turned the corner to our apartment—and Marius was standing there.

Before I could utter a sound, he had his hand across my mouth, carrying me to the other stairwell that led to the parking lot exit. I kicked and fought as hard as I could, but he was monstrous when he was angry. Before I could recall a single self defense move Abel had taught me, I found my wrists zip tied together and feet secured with rope in the front seat of the car Marius already had running.

Desperately looking out the window as we pulled away, I wondered how I found myself once again abducted and restrained by this awful human I deeply loved only yesterday. I caught a glimpse of Abel and Ruth running from the apartment building toward the getaway car. Abel kept running far too long. I wondered if he actually thought he would catch us, and at the same time hoped he wouldn't give up. It seemed like chasing down a moving vehicle was an impossible thing to do, but I believed that if Abel didn't quit, he probably could catch us. But then, as I knew he would have to, he stopped running. I watched him let go of his stride and fall back, putting his hands on his knees and breathing like the air burned his lungs.

We moved farther and farther away from Abel and Ruth. I saw Abel run, possibly faster, in the opposite direction. Although I felt a sense of dread wash over me the further we separated from my freedom, I knew something that I didn't know before, which allowed me to hold onto hope. I will visit my dad. I had to be alive to do that. The possibility that what we did on this time travel could alter future events in a negative way nagged in the back of my mind but I refused to entertain that scenario.

CHAPTER 14

RUTH

I knew that girl like the back of my hand. As soon as Taden took off toward the door, I knew where she was headed. She could not let this night repeat history. After all Taden had accomplished, she still couldn't figure out how to fix her feelings connected to this night. But there was a madman out there who also knew how badly Taden wanted this reparation, and he had already put her in danger once. We were not sure what he wanted and it wasn't worth her safety to make amends with our mom's death and my drug addiction.

"Abel! Taden's leaving! Back door! Hurry!" He was outside before I said *hurry*. I returned to Dr. Pasterski and made sure she was okay. I told her, "Lock the front and back door. Do *not* let anyone in under any circumstances. Sit with your phone until I return, just in case Taden calls you." Then I ran home as fast as my legs would move.

Taden was just barely in the lead.

We rounded the corner from the top of the stairs after her, to find she was gone. How could she disappear into thin air? I ran to our door and pounded on it, yelling, "Taden? Open up!" Ruth pulled open the door, staring at me wide-eyed. In desperation, I asked her, "Did you just let a woman in?" With concern she shook her head no.

However, she informed me, "That doctor from the picture you showed me was just knocking on my door a few minutes ago. I didn't answer it. I saw him through the window and had a bad feeling, since you two had been here asking about him. Then, he left, carrying a woman that way." She pointed to the other exit.

Abel jolted down the hall to the back stairwell. By the time we got outside, Marius was peeling out of the dimly lit parking lot in a rusted car, Taden in the passenger seat. She pressed her hands, tied together, against the window as they pulled away.

Abel ran after them at a frantic pace. I cupped my hands to my mouth. "Abel! Come back!"

Thankfully, he gave up his dog chase after the fleeing car. He needed another second to catch his breath. Before he began to speak, I started with my suggestion. "We need a car to catch up with them! Dr. Pasterski has one we can use."

He closed his eyes momentarily, appearing like he might cry. Before I could be certain that's what I saw, it was gone and he was back into Superman mode. He already decided on his idea of what would happen next.

"Ruth, go back to Dr. Pasterski. You need to make sure she's okay and stick with her until I return. I'm going after your sister to bring her back safe."

Of course I wasn't going to accept this plan of his! "There is no way I am staying here and letting you go after Taden alone!"

"I. Am not. Asking you. This a government matter, Ruth. If you cooperate and go sit with Dr. Pasterski, I can focus all of my attention on Taden and feel confident that Dr. Pasterski is also being kept safe. We don't know what Marius is up to and who he could be working with. I am beginning to suspect he might be here as a part of the terrorist activities happening at home. His meddling with time could put Dr. Pasterski in danger. We don't know the ramifications of our time traveling yet. Go back Ruth. Please. She has a gun in her lab for protection. It was there when Taden and I used to assist her with lab work. I am counting on it to be something she possessed before that time. If so, have her get it out. She will know how to use it."

Every second he spent trying to convince me of what needed to be done was another second Marius was getting further away with my sister.

"Okay. I get it. Go! Hurry!" I pushed him, to show I agreed he should leave. He broke into a car parked in the lot and had it started before I was even on my way to Dr. Pasterski's.

Walking back in the twilight, my thoughts wrestled between how I should have never left my sister alone and if it would have changed a thing. If I hadn't, she would not have fallen so deep into this trap with Marius. I would have seen right through him from the start. But then, who was I kidding? When has reason ever stopped someone from falling in love with the wrong person?

When I got back to Dr. Pasterski's house, I updated her with what had just happened to Taden and everything I knew about Marius, which wasn't much, except he was bad news. I explained that Abel instructed us to stay here with her supposed gun and wait.

With that, she rather quickly retrieved her gun from the lab. A part of me didn't believe that she owned a gun, let alone knew how to use it. It was hard enough to believe she was a part of a secret government organization to overthrow our current system and defend the country against a national takeover, but there she was, gun in hand, perfectly comfortable with the idea of using it. I caught myself staring at her in a stunned silence.

"Ruth, I'm sure you are bewildered. I can't imagine how you are processing all of this." She held up her gun to show that she understood even this minor part was difficult for me to digest. "I think we both need to relax our nerves a bit. Let's go make some tea and sit in the kitchen. We can listen better to the neighborhood in there with the windows open, and also keep an eye on your apartment building to see if there's anything suspicious in that direction. We should be looking out for the two little girls over there," she said as she winked at me.

I almost forgot about the two little girls about to lose their mother. The protective big sister in me wanted to go over there this instant and tell myself not to let Taden leave tonight. But then I thought about the time travel aspect. How could my interference make a mess of things? The little bit that Abel said about us not fully understanding the ramifications. It made me think, just by being here we could be altering our lives in so many ways big and small. Nothing is guaranteed just because it was what we knew when we left. The longer we stay, the more changes made, the bigger the ripple could be when we return home. I decided I probably shouldn't be interfering with any events, however badly I wanted to, when I didn't totally understand the outcomes.

I did realize, however, that I should give Dr. Pasterski a heads up about Taden on her way over to the lab. "Dr. Pasterski, I don't know if you remember this, but you told young Taden she could come over tonight to work on something you two have been cooking up. She'll probably be here any minute now. Should I hide somewhere, or should you cancel with her?" I asked, still wanting to save my sister a lifetime of regret by not coming here tonight even though my brain already logically spelled out the consequences.

"This is the night then, isn't it?" She raised an eyebrow. Sometimes it seemed impossible to get anything past her.

"Yes, this is the night." I hung my head low, grief bubbling up toward the surface. "Taden isn't home when it happens. She was still here, finishing up her work. I know we shouldn't change this but I so wish we could. We can't keep her from coming here tonight? Will it affect too much? Taden spent so much time with her regret. If you tell her not to come, she will be home when it happens."

Dr. Pasterski lowered her head and looked at me as a mother does when she knows her child is hurting but cannot stop it. "You know we can't change this for your sister. She must decide for herself the path that she will take. The timelines that she will travel. I can only hope that Taden discovers the truth in her heart and allows her past to be, for it is what made her the woman that she is."

Her response, although I perfectly understood it, was as difficult to hear as seeing her hold a gun. I wanted to be angry with her. It seemed so selfish that a lifetime of regret was worth time travel. But also, I understood what Dr. Pasterski was saying. It was a lifetime of achievement. If I took away her regret, I could possibly be taking away her achievement with it. It really wasn't my choice to make on behalf of my sister, but it was still my decision to let the teenage version of her leave our apartment tonight and miss saying goodbye to Mom. I didn't know if I could ever tell her I did that.

Surrendering my query for a new one I asked, "So if she's coming here, should I go hide somewhere? Should I pretend to be someone else? What do you think?"

She thought for a minute and decided, "No, I think we both stay in here. The work she is doing this evening is independent from me. She has already begun the task, and will not even need to know I am home. I'll leave her a note." Dr. Pasterski got up to write a short note informing Taden she was gone and to lock up after she was done. "She is such a responsible and dependable young lady." I had known this was true about Taden since she was a little girl.

I could still see her innocent, freckled face look up at me with her big blue eyes, telling me about how she was going to help Dad build a car. In true Taden fashion, she carefully explained that first she had to learn about how cars work, holding out the stack of library books she had just gotten with Mom. Her dark auburn hair was separated in twin braids that she asked me to put in every single morning before school.

People never saw a resemblance between me and Taden unless they compared us to our mother. We both always heard how much we looked like her. I think it was deeper than what we looked like. I think people could subconsciously sense our mother within us. They saw her on our faces.

 We sat in Dr. Pasterski's kitchen, quietly listening and anxiously waiting. First, we waited for young Taden to arrive to complete her work in the lab. After she arrived, we listened harder for any sign of Marius returning, because then we had adult Taden to worry about.

We didn't think *his* return to be likely, since he already had adult Taden in his grip. However, we didn't know if Marius was working with anyone else, and if so, if *they* would be coming for us. Still, we listened hardest for Abel.

If Abel was to return, so would Taden, and everything would be alright. The longer we waited, the more tense we became.

After a few hours, we heard Taden leave the lab and head home. This meant my younger self was about to face my mom leaving the Earth. I could feel my throat tighten up, and my eyes begin to burn. About ten minutes after she went home, we could hear sobbing in the street. I almost forgot that she took off that night upon discovering Mom had died, and I had to leave my mom's body to run after Taden.

It was instantaneous how my grief and dismay of my mom having just died turned to worry and fear that something might happen to my sister after she hysterically ran out.

I closed my eyes in an attempt to stop myself from crying, pursed my lips together, and took a deep breath in through my nose. When I opened them back up, I told Dr. Pasterski, "That's Taden out there. She just walked in to find our mom had already passed on. She's out in the street crying. We need to go to her. This can't be something that will alter our timelines? To comfort her out there alone on the street? I'll stay back a bit and try to be inconspicuous." Dr. Pasterski looked perplexed. She didn't seem convinced that she should go out to Taden. Her hesitance was too much for me to bear while hearing the screaming agony from my sister outside. "I'll go myself if you don't come with me. I refuse to leave her out there alone."

"You're right, dear. Let's go to her now. The consequence of this action cannot possibly outweigh the consequence of our inaction here." We ran out to Taden and found her in a heap on the sidewalk. Dr. Pasterski helped her up, comforting her, "Shhh. I know darling. It's going to be alright. I know."

We weren't there very long before teenage Ruth joined us. She looked destroyed. I wanted to go to her. I wanted to tell her the same words that Dr. Pasterski was giving to Taden. But I couldn't. They were lies. Everything wasn't alright, and it wouldn't be for a long time. This Ruth needed to be the strong one, and I knew it. So I let her. Instead, I held onto those words of comfort for myself. My present self.

I helped Dr. Pasterski lift Taden up, and the two of us walked her back home. Ruth followed behind us. I knew what she was thinking. I remembered all of it. It's funny that younger me never wondered what "Maria" was doing there with Dr. Pasterski after meeting her with Abel. All along, that random woman there that night was actually *me*. I wondered briefly if I had ever encountered other future versions of myself throughout my life without knowing.

Standing in the apartment, yet again, it was all I could do to avoid looking at my mom lying there, gone. I had already lived through this scene one time too many.

Inside, I felt like a toddler about to melt down into a full-blown tantrum. I shouldn't have been here for this. Taden and Ruth did not need some random woman falling apart in their living room after losing their mother.

I tried to breathe through the attack of anguish, but flashes of what would come next kept taking center stage. Her body would be wheeled out of the house. I would see her in a casket after that. Then she would be in an urn, just a pile of ashes. I had to get out of there.

I excused myself from the scene and headed back to Dr. Pasterski's, where I would be a lot better off keeping watch for my sister.

During the brisk walk back to her house again that evening, I wished more than anything that Taden was with me. My Taden, adult Taden. She was the only person that understood the impact of this night and how much torture it was. It was particularly awful that this was the night we had been forced to relive through Taden's time traveling.

In wishing for her, I was able to once again switch out my grief for my mom with worrying about my sister. Of the two human emotions, worrying felt better than grief.

I let the worry take hold of me, planting myself next to Dr. Pasterski's phone and watched it intensely, willing Taden to call.

CHAPTER 15

TADEN

Terror built up inside of me, but not because of Marius. He could do whatever he wanted with me. I didn't care anymore. This was a different terror, one I already knew well. I was about to lose my mom all over again. This was the night. I had a choice to make.

Sitting in his car, tied up once more, I looked over at another wrong choice I had made. Marius. *How could I have been so stupid?* After all he had done, it was still hard for me to understand how another human could be completely void of empathy. *How could a living, breathing soul sit so close to me, see the pain and torment I was in, and feel nothing of it? Not even a pang of guilt?*

It wouldn't make a difference, but I begged him one more time to let me go back and say goodbye. "Marius, I don't know why you are doing this but I haven't done anything to you but love you. You know what this night means to me. Please just let me go back and fix my mistake, then you can do whatever you want with me."

Then I wondered, what *did* he want with me? Looking over his face for some flicker of the Marius I believed in for so long, I saw nothing. He didn't even have the capability of pretending, like "Dr. Touma," that he cared.

In fact, it was starting to seem like *I* was his target of anger and hatred. It was *me* who he wanted to destroy. I couldn't fathom what I had done to him to make him so hellbent on hurting me. "What do you want from me, Marius? Just tell me. I don't care what it is. You can have it. All I want is to see my mom."

Thick with condescension, he laughed at me, rolling his eyes and shaking his head at my ignorance. This was when I first entertained what I had slightly suspected: *could he be a part of this takeover?*

"I came to the United States from my home in Iraq as a teenager. In the refugee camps I stayed in along the way, I made connections with people who had big plans for me. They could see my potential and wanted me to join them in their movement they called The Reckoning. Eventually, I was granted citizenship—which was nearly impossible, even *with* the right people pulling strings for me. Following the directions my people gave me and excelling, I eventually worked my way into a government role. During this seed-planting phase of the The Reckoning, many other rebel agents also settled into your government to position themselves. Over the last two decades we watched as your government sabotaged itself. Once the strongest in the world, it began to eat itself from within. When it was time, we decided to make our move. The Reckoners did nothing but wait for the day that our plan to finish your failed democracy could be executed."

I couldn't help but replay every moment we had shared together. From my initial interview with him when I decided to hire him onto my team, our kiss on that first all-nighter, the many moments we lie in bed together. None of it was real. I had been living a lie with this man. "Why did you commit me into a mental hospital? Was that just some sick and twisted fun you were having?"

"Actually, it seemed like the most kind way to get you to tell me everything I needed to know. If I could coerce you to believe you were having delusions and trust me with helping you sort them from reality, I felt certain you would reveal to me in detail all of your ideas in notebooks. Which would include your serum. It would have been like stealing candy from a baby."

My mouth gaped open. Not sure how I could still be shocked by anything. He used me to complete his agenda. They wanted time travel to have complete control over the outcome of their will. Somewhere in our timelines, they found out I would have this technology to take. Worse than that, I opened the door to him, and now The Reckoners who had attacked our country would get what they want. They were going to take it from me, and with it they would be able to change events to their benefit.

Although it felt extremely self-pitying, I also noted that I had just discovered a similar truth with Abel. Even if he was the "good guy" to Marius's "bad guy" it still felt like he was lying to me all these years, too. And there it was, a woe-is-me moment to succumb to. I let my mind and my emotions center around the thought that two of the most important relationships I carried on with in the last decade had been a cover.

Suddenly, I felt violently sick and threw up on the floor of the passenger seat. Marius flinched and pulled his face in disgust as the smell sifted into the air. Then he turned to look away from me out his driver's side window while rolling it down to breathe in the outside.

At that moment, I was more disgusted with Marius than he was with my vomit. I realized he was taking me somewhere that I actually might *not* live through.

My initial thought about visiting my dad in the past made me feel safe from this present danger, but then I doubted the certainty of that outcome. That path is what will happen with all choices as they were at the moment Dr. Pasterski told me of the visit with Dad. I was questioning though if I veered off the path that led to that outcome, if a new choice in this timeline was to be made that wasn't made originally, if it might change that outcome completely. Marius could turn and kill me dead right here in this car, something he didn't do in the timeline that led to me seeing my dad, and therefore, the outcome will have changed. Nothing is guaranteed or written in stone. Any choice could alter our timeline. With these theories taking hold in my thoughts, I tried to focus on where Marius must have been taking me.

He was not going to kill me in the car. He was taking me to the beginning of The Reckoning. *I* was what they needed to win this war and throw us into anarchy. I could give them a power that no one could challenge. I could give them the past to rewrite. I could not let him succeed in handing me over. I had to fight. Contrary to what I had said to him moments before out of desperation to get back to my mom, I wouldn't be giving him whatever he wanted. I would not be his victim. I certainly would not be his accomplice. I was made for more.

I had been trained for this. Abel saw to that. He knew I was going to need combat training, and he believed I was strong enough to fight this battle. It struck me that he probably also knew about Marius long before today. He made sure that even though Marius objected to my training, I received it and could defend myself.

Of course Marius didn't want me to be able to fight. He was my antagonist and I would be fighting *him*. Looking at him, I felt disgust and a desire to destroy him and everything he stood for. When I found my voice again, I asked, "So where are you taking me?"

"We are going to see some people I know who would love to talk to you." He laughed. "You know what? They wouldn't need to talk to you at all if it wasn't for your brilliant decision to cypher the data with Dakotah. Luckily you seem more willing to cooperate with us than I thought you were going to be. I should have known you would offer up your life's work just for one goodbye with your mom. You can be so predictable, Taden. But who knows, if you're impressive enough, The Reckoners may invite you to work for me. In *my* time travel department." He smiled like he had won a childhood game.

I was watching him tell me his plan, and I couldn't see anything attractive about his face. I knew that I felt differently mere hours ago, but it was almost like the attraction I felt had been erased from time.

His dark eyes were no longer mysteriously intriguing; I found them to be filled with malice and contempt. His dimpled smile didn't make my face flush with longing. Instead, my face reddened with fury. I didn't see his body as a safe place to weather any storm. He carried a body of destruction and danger. At that moment, I felt the shift of power I had lost to him the night of our first kiss come back to me.

With a sudden surge, I declared my true intent to him. "I am only willing to cooperate with you if you take me back to say goodbye. You know she is going to die tonight. What would you do if you knew this was your last chance to say goodbye to your sister the night she died?"

I tried using his sister's death to remind him of our shared loss, hoping this last attempt to get him to take me back to my mom would work. That maybe bringing up his sister would remind him of our connection, even though I felt nauseous at the thought of being connected to this monster. The loss we both experienced in our lives used to be an unspeakable bond—or so he let me believe.

"Don't you *ever* mention my sister to me again. You think I *won't* see her? I have news for you, Taden, I will. I will become the father of time travel. I will go to her and save her from the death she was handed from *your* government." He sounded like a raving lunatic.

My government? It seemed like he believed I was somehow responsible for his sister's death. It should also not have surprised me (but it did) that his sister was killed. I was fed the story that she got sick and died from complications caused by her illness.

As he talked about his sister, he did frighten me a little. A *sane* Marius could be scary, but it was obvious that he was far from sane. He turned his head sharply toward me, taking his eyes off the road, while he continued to drive frantically toward my demise.

With accusation in his voice, he asked, "You think I'm the bad guy don't you? Of course you do. Your simple brain only sees what it wants, doesn't it? That's why it was so easy to make you believe in Marius, your true love." He spat his words toward me. They no longer pierced my heart. His ranting continued. "My sister was trying to flee from the dangers in our country. There was war and death. They were hurting women and young girls in ways that I could *never* allow to happen to her. She came to this country for asylum, and it handed her death. This country doesn't deserve its freedom, and I swear it won't have it. It won't have my sister's life either."

I wanted him to refocus on the road but instead he looked at me as though *I* was his sister's murderer. It was an awful story. For a brief minute, I honestly felt rage *with* Marius for his sister. It wasn't the story he told me originally, so it was hard to know if it was the truth or not, but it did seem like the kind of truth that would drive a person to become a madman like Marius. Maybe *I* would be the same way if the roles were reversed and I was avenging my father.

While I thought I could understand why Marius had gone down the path he chose, it didn't make me hate him any less for it.

We drove in silence that screamed the resentment we felt for each other. I used this reprieve for plotting how I would maneuver my impending meeting with the original Reckoners. What I did at that meeting would determine the future of my country—and hell, it would determine what would happen with my time travel discoveries and possibly my survival.

I wasn't going to fight my way out of this, even if I had been somewhat trained in self-defense. I was going to need to use my brain and come up with an actionable plan. I needed to abandon the idea of trying to persuade Marius from taking me to my mom first and then escaping, because now I understood that this was bigger than me and my mom. This was intel that the Patriot Party needed. I could be the source to find out who the key players were and where they could be located. This is what my Dad died trying to accomplish.

Immediately, I started paying attention to where we were and where we were going. I would need to be careful to listen for names and collect detailed descriptions of what each person looked like. Then I set on brainstorming how I would exit once I had gotten all the imperative information I could—which led me to the serum.

I was wearing a timed-release band when I traveled back here with Marius. Even though he talked me into leaving with him to say goodbye to my mom without the consent of the Patriot Party, we still took the agreed upon protocol. *Of course!* The serum! I decided I might have the start of a pretty good plan in place. "Marius, what did you do with my timed-release band? I had it on when we traveled here, but clearly you took it off me in the mental institution."

He laughed at me and retorted, "Right. First of all *why* would I tell you that? Second of all, no kidding I took it off you!"

Annoyed, I sharply responded, "You're taking me to a group of people who want me to tell them everything they need to know to complete time travel. I need the serum to break apart the mixture in order to recreate more of it for them. I can't start from nothing." I was lying. I knew breaking apart this mixture would be next to impossible.

The thing was, this was not Marius's area of expertise. His strength was found when using and testing existing science. Asking him to figure out what is in the serum, reproduce it, or to figure out how much would be needed to stimulate time travel would take a lifetime for him to solve. I knew this about him, no matter what lies he had told me about everything else. I was beginning to feel that this was what he hated so much about me. Either way, this was my angle: to play on his weakness.

Feeling confident, I asked him, "You do have your timed-release band don't you? It would be pretty stupid for you to bring me here and not have either of ours with you." I was poking the bear, not letting my fear of him take over. I knew he was massively insecure about the fact that I was smarter than him, so, I decided to use it for my benefit.

Marius flared his nose and sucked in his breath at my slight toward him. He sneered. "I have them both, *actually*. I'm not an *idiot*. I'm not going to just hand them over to you. I can see you are trying to get out of here. If you do need the serum to create more for us, then I will be sure you have access to it in a laboratory under careful monitoring."

It was a little disappointing that he wasn't as much of a dumbass as I had hoped he was, but it was enough to get him to admit that both bands were here in the car with us. I just had to figure out where they were and get my hands on at least one of them. Plus, if Abel was still trying to find me he could use the tracker Dakotah embedded into the timed-release bands. I believed he would at least attempt it, because he was the one who suggested she add them to her design, and Marius wasn't at that meeting. He decided not to come because he was busy with the data readings that morning. He had no idea that by having those bands in the car with us, Abel could find us. I just had to have faith that Abel was still looking and hadn't gone back to the present with Ruth, having left me here in the past.

Eventually, we turned down a road. After a few miles the pavement stopped and we were traveling on dirt. I could sense that we were almost there.

Pulling into the driveway of a tiny, run down house, I found myself slightly disappointed. I had worked up in my mind a fantastically awful place, a giant, sterile building that could be seen on *The X-Files.*

Instead, it appeared we were heading into a meth lab. The rundown rickety shack of a house was almost hidden by overgrown fields and bushes. Roof tiles were hanging on in a last effort before blowing away in the next storm and window panes appeared as if they would crumble to the touch. It threw me off. Marius parked the car and jumped out of his seat. He walked around the front and zeroed his eyes in on me as he approached my passenger door. *Did he think I would apparate out of the seat before his very eyes?* After he opened my door, he instructed me, "Sit tight a minute. I have some things to get from the trunk, and then I'll escort you inside."

I had to stop letting my mind remember who I believed Marius to be just this morning. I could see yesterday's Marius say the same thing to me after we arrived at our bed and breakfast trip over a summer holiday break. It was a sensory memory my brain recalled without my permission. It did not come attached with any feelings of love or loss. It made me want to vomit again. I shook my head to rid myself of the false narrative I had for him. Briefly, I wished I was a scholar in memory wiping.

Through the dark, I caught a reflection of Marius in the side mirror pulling out a duffle bag. I was certain he had the timed-release bands in it. I would need to be aware of where he set that bag down. He walked back around to me with my door still open and reached in to grab my arms, still zip tied together.

Standing in the beam of the car headlights that hadn't turned off yet, I asked, "Are you going to undo this? You know perfectly well that I have no way out of wherever we are and that it is pointless for me to be tied up. Especially since I am going to be working for you in there." He was in a rush to get inside, and I knew his adrenaline was pumping. "I think it will look better for you, Marius, if it appears you got me here somewhat willingly rather than taking me in like a prisoner you will have to force to cooperate. Don't you?"

He thought about what I told him for a minute, which I believed was the most consideration he gave me all day. Then he said, "You do have a point there, Tay. My people *will* be impressed if, even after I revealed myself to you, you still want to be with me." This made my insides turn to ash that churned and burned, threatening to ignite into a raging fire.

He pulled a knife out of his pants and swiftly had the zip ties cut and the rope around my feet off. After returning his knife to his pants, he grabbed my arm with his free hand and forcefully escorted me inside.

The inside of the house looked exactly like I pictured it based on my first impression of the outside. There was next to nothing in the sparsely-lit house besides some tables and chairs strewn about. It gave the impression that the only thing that happened in this dingy dwelling were gatherings of people who met for planning then got the hell out. I noticed a dark hallway to my right with three closed doors, but we didn't go that way.

Instead, he walked me through the desolate living room and into the kitchen (that appeared to serve as another meeting room), then toward the stairs I assumed led to a basement. I was pushed forward to start down the stairs first, and Marius followed so close behind I could feel his breath on my neck. It motivated me to walk faster. Halfway down the stairs, I could hear several voices and see a dangling lightbulb glowing. The voices sounded like they belonged only to men. My discomfort rose. I was suddenly the only woman among a group of men that I already knew to be, at the core, not good.

Marius and I stopped at the bottom of the stairs. Three men stared up at us from another table surrounded by chairs. Whatever they were discussing quickly died off when we entered the basement. I was already busy collecting every detail of every face.

Upon my first impression, I noticed I was looking at three men who seemed to be from three different parts of the world. It was like a meeting of delegates. They did appear to be speaking the same language, though I wasn't sure which, at first.

The younger, dark-skinned man to my left was in an all-black suit, yet adorned with gold jewelry: chunky rings on his fingers, a thick, chain link bracelet, and a large rope necklace with a pendant that contained some kind of middle eastern script. He wore a striking, boxed beard and mustache. The jet black hair on his head was slicked back in a high pompadour.

To my right sat a much older Asian man who appeared like an important politician in his navy suit paired with a crisp white shirt and red tie. His graying hair was kept in a classically-parted comb over. I could imagine his impeccably-shaved face was regularly cared for by a personal barber. On his ring finger, he wore a golden band, the only of the three who appeared to be married. It made him seem less dangerous than the other two.

The last man, directly in front of me, looked to be in his late 50s with his full head of gray hair. He was in the best physical shape of the three. I expect that his longer, straight, side-swept hair was once blond, to go with his fair skin and blue eyes. A long face held his high, wide cheekbones and square jaw. He too was cleanly shaven, and wore no tie with his navy blue jacket on top of a navy button-up shirt.

After taking in the details I could see, I listened more carefully as they spoke to each other. It was surprising to figure out that they *were* speaking English. They each had thick accents, so they were difficult to understand. I tried to figure out where I thought each man was from.

The buffer-looking guy instructed me to sit down. I obeyed, then turned my study upon him. He took the lead, so I assumed he must have some role of power in this summit.

I would not show any fear to these men. Instead, they would get the self-assured scientist character I'm so good at portraying. I sat tall and opened my arms widely across the table to take up more space that I inherently owned. My body language said *I dare you,* even if my thoughts told me to run and hide. All this dramatic effect for nothing. He didn't even look at me, but turned his icy blue eyes on Marius, who couldn't have seemed more proud of himself if he wanted to.

He was waiting for them to pin a medal into his chest that very second. However, Marius's moment of glory was pulled out from underneath him.

"Why did you bring this woman here? Do you value your life so little? Protocol is to be followed, Marius," he chided him.

I could not take my eyes off the man that threatened Marius. He was the first human I had ever witnessed dismiss him without so much of a blink of an eye. Even people I knew who didn't like Marius dared not insult his credibility. It was humbling to watch, but then it concerned me that if it was so easy for *him* to be discounted by this man, *I* would have no chance here.

None of the men were glaring at me with contempt any longer, but had traded their gazes onto Marius. I joined them. It was fascinating to watch him respond to this interrogation. He cleared his throat and looked back at me. I suppose I was his easiest critic in the room at that point.

"Gentlemen, this is Dr. Taden Barrett. She is our number one. I have brought her to you, of her own free will, to give you time travel. She knows of The Reckoning, since it has already begun in our present. Dr. Barrett is joining our fight, men," Marius finished with a gleaming smile. I had to bite back the bile rising up in my throat.

They all returned their watchful eyes to me. Seconds turned into minutes, which felt like hours that we sat in silence. I looked over each man's face again and again. I was aware they were waiting on me to speak first. I decided I would exert my power by remaining silent and let the onus of the conversation fall to them.

Marius broke the silence, "Dr. Barrett, explain to these men how you can help them."

His words were spoken as a command through gritted teeth, over which he plastered a smile. I swallowed hard and continued my silence. If I died refusing to make the first move here, so be it. It was the only way I could foresee that I would be able to have any dignity or respect.

Again, the man across from me spoke. This time I side-glanced at the other two, looking for any sign of their participation in this meeting. They just watched and listened to the speaking of their apparent superior. Through his thick accent, I could detect a Scandanavian dialect. I confidently pinpointed him to be from Norway or Sweden.

He addressed me with his sing-song accent, "Dr. Barrett? Marius here boasts that you have sent humans back into time. Is this correct?" I nodded in response to his question. "He also tells us that you have coded all your data, so he has been unable to replicate what you have done. Impressive."

I granted the tiniest smile to crease along my mouth. He raised his eyebrows in return. If I was reading this man correctly, he seemed to distaste Marius more than he did me. This was not a terrible sign.

I decided I would engage with and convince him I had what he needed. I've done this before with my people, the Patriots included. "Sir, I have spent the entirety of my adult life discovering and fine-tuning human time travel. I am confident in my abilities, and am quite capable of replicating my data given the proper materials. Marius has my serum in his duffle bag and I would be happy to start my work immediately."

I looked over at Marius with a poisonous smile. He returned an equally vexing look to me. He no longer had any control over my feelings and emotions. This resulted in what appeared to be shock regarding the lack of pain he could supply to me. My new power move wasn't foreseen. It was clear he didn't want to fumble, so he pulled out the bands from his bag. I was impressed with myself.

"Here is the serum Dr. Barrett has requested in order to replicate more for you, but I would feel more comfortable keeping it in my possession."

The tall man in charge responded to Marius. "Are you concerned with Dr. Barrett's intentions?"

It was a loaded question. If Marius had answered that he did doubt me, it would again make him look bad for bringing me here but if he answered that he didn't doubt me they would want to know why he felt the need to keep the serum on his person. I could tell he was sweating this answer. I took the lead here. For once, Marius would not win over the crowd. I would, and this was necessary more now than ever.

"Excuse me sir, if I may speak?" I looked at him for permission to continue and he nodded his approval. I glanced over at Marius and his eyes were wide with disbelief. I felt proud that he could be so decidedly wrong about the strength of my presence. "Thank you. I am quite sure Marius feels protective of the timed-release band, as do I. I assure you that you do not have to be concerned with me having access to it, as I am the person who created the serum to begin with. It wouldn't be impossible for me to start over from the beginning if Marius decided he did not want me to have access to the band. That's okay if this is what you decide, as well. However, it might take many months—possibly up to a year for me to start over. With the serum Marius has in his hand right now, I could have replications made at an exponentially faster rate. Of course, it is up to you gentleman how you choose to proceed. I will obviously support whatever decision you make." I smiled complacently and watched Marius squirm under my authority once again. He closed his eyes to hide the painful blow.

"Marius, what do you think we should do in response to Dr. Barrett?" The man asked. If he answered honestly, it would reveal the heart of who he was. I've seen his core, and it was nothing but power hungry and self-serving.

He was smart enough to play his cards right. He replied, "I certainly agree that if Dr. Barrett can replicate the serum in that short amount of time she should not be asked to start from the beginning."

But then he regained momentum and the look that appeared across his face revealed he wasn't in checkmate yet. He reached into his bag and pulled out a timed-release band while dropping the bag to the ground. With both hands, Marius tore open the band and removed the serum from within. I watched in horror as my immediate chance at escape was snatched from me. Pleased with his last second upset, he handed me my serum vial. Speechless, I reached out to accept it.

I wasn't going to get stuck in this moment hanging onto a minor loss. Once I was in a lab working, it wouldn't be impossible to get the vial into a syringe. I couldn't see that I would be left alone or that it would be simple to accomplish but it was a possibility. I just had to get to a syringe before I was forced to empty the serum to begin the process of separating the mixture. Mentally noting that there was still one timed-release band intact within Marius's bag, I continued gathering details and filing them into my memory.

"Thank you!" I said holding up the vial to the men at the table and back at Marius. "I'm ready to start working as soon as you have somewhere for me to do that."

The ringleader slowly folded his hands and brought them to his thin lips as he watched me with the vial. He looked to Marius now, and gave him instructions in another language I wasn't familiar with. It wasn't Arabic which Marius spoke as a first language. I was somewhat familiar with this language listening to him speak it and practicing on my own when I could. I didn't recognize any of the pacing or words the two men were communicating with in their short exchange.

I could tell from the tone in Marius's response that whatever he was being told, he didn't like. He kept side-glancing me with the disgusted face I'd come to expect whenever he looked at me. It caught me off guard that Marius knew another language besides Arabic. This was an important reminder that he wasn't as dumb as I would like to think he was, and I should not be underestimating him.

After they finished speaking, Marius abruptly grabbed his duffle bag and retreated back up the stairs. I could hear his heavy footsteps cross the kitchen floor and disappear in the distance. I took a deep breath and held onto my tough exterior, returning my eye contact directly onto each of these men. I heard Marius refer to the ringleader as Vergard in his attempts to dissuade him from whatever he was directing him to do. He once again turned his attention to me.

"So, Dr. Barrett, while Marius is out running a quick errand, let's get to know you a bit better." I nodded my head slightly to show approval at his request. "How long have you been aware of Marius's role here with us?"

"Only today."

"How do you feel about this betrayal?"

"I feel about it as one might any betrayal. I was unpleasantly surprised to learn I was sharing my life with a man who was not who he said he was. I am over the shock now. It is what it is." I shrugged my shoulders to convey I had not been broken in soul or spirit by their comrade.

"Why would you agree to work with him against all you stand for in light of these revelations of his character?"

"Sir, if I may speak plainly?" I waited for his approval to continue. He resumed his earlier posture with both index fingers meeting as if representing a temple resting on his upper lip. Once he raised his chin at me, a sign to continue, I spoke. "I am motivated to produce what you need because I understand it makes me valuable to you. In other words, it makes me not dead." A smile parted his thin lips revealing stark-white teeth. Vergard didn't fully give me the creeps until that smile took hold of him. I swallowed to hide my waver in strength. The older Asian man interjected for the first time.

"Ms. Barrett, you can call me Feng. We knew your father. He sat across from us as you do now. Unfortunately, he did not feel the same as you in regards to working with us."

My mouth went dry. Of course, this must be where he was taken to be killed. By these men most likely. It's funny how much rage can swirl through a person so quickly. I was a burning fire.

"My father did have his convictions. They didn't seem to do him or anyone else any good though. Did they?"

"You are correct Ms. Barrett. He did not choose very wisely. We gave him plenty of time to change his mind. Day after day, he would sit, where you sit now, and refuse us. It was most disappointing." As he said this to me, he too allowed an evil smile to creep across his face. "As a matter of fact, Ms. Barrett, while you are working with us, you will be in the very room your father stayed in while he was with us. That should be…comforting for you, yes?"

I nodded my head once and moved my gaze from his face to the table. My teeth ground together and my hands pulled into fists. I took a deep breath and returned the placid smile to my face, turning my attention back to Vergard. He was uninterested in the exchange between Feng and me.

Vergard asked the third man about Marius upstairs. I was confused for a moment, because I was sure they had just sent him on an errand. Feng maintained his watch of me and it began to feel incredibly unsettling. The conversation about Marius developed enough that I was able to clarify that the *young* version of Marius was upstairs in one of those bedrooms.

He had recently arrived in the country. They were hosting him until they could obtain more permanent living arrangements. It was fascinating to think that the most pivotal moment in Marius's life was underway right upstairs.

Of course, I couldn't resist considering the heroic storyline I could play in attempting to thwart this path of his life. Shaking my head slightly to rid myself of this need to fix Marius, I refocused on what they were discussing. It appeared that my Marius—well, not *my* Marius, but the adult Marius—just found out his counterpart was here as well, and was sent to get the boy version some food. The men did not want the two versions of themselves to meet out of fear that it could cause some type of unforeseen issue that might change their mission. They did not understand the laws of time travel experiences but they did have a background of human ideas about time travel through popular culture. They felt particular concern about the two Marius's meeting even though there were no scientific grounds to have concern about this event occurring. I didn't feel particularly obliged to ease their concerns either.

Marius was angry about not being able to see himself. I could understand. I had my own desire to come face to face with the younger version of myself to depart some wisdom. Hell, I was just entertaining the idea with the younger version of Marius. Of course he wanted to meet his younger self. At that thought, I knew Marius hadn't left the house. My mind replayed hearing him up the stairs and into the kitchen above us, but I didn't hear him leave the house yet. I recalled that when we came into the house the screen door slammed shut behind us. Besides, if Marius had already made up his mind to do something, no one could tell him no. I made my play.

"Pardon me, I apologize for interrupting. I couldn't help but listen to your discussion about young Marius not meeting his adult counterpart. I have to tell you that your concern might be met right now. I'm quite certain he did not leave. I'm sure you will find him up in the boy's room at this very moment."

"That is a strong accusation, Ms. Barrett. It appears maybe you do hold some resentment for your scorned love?"

His comment was revolting, but I made a deal with myself not to react to these men in an emotional manner. "Suit yourself, gentlemen. I was merely trying to point out a valid concern on your behalf. What harm would going upstairs to inquire of my accusation cause?"

With the challenge placed, they couldn't sit idly by and ignore the possible disregard for their commands that Marius may have breached. "Jaali, go," Vergard commanded. The man who had spoken nothing to me stood to his feet and bounded up the stairs in four strides. The three of us sat in tense quiet. Then, pounding on the bedroom door, followed by his command to open it. Thumping and banging sounds made it clear that a struggle was taking place. Neither Vergard or Feng seemed rattled. They continued to sit and wait.

I tried my best to mirror their composure. I wanted to bite my lips, chew my nails, tap my foot, pace the floor. Any of my desired behaviors would appear weak to these men. Before long, the banging came tumbling down the stairs. Jaali dragged adult Marius down each step.

The level of credibility Marius had lost with this act of defiance, transferred right over to me. I was feeling quite smug and again had to recenter myself into an illegibly calm exterior.

"Impressive, Ms. Barrett. You know your lover better than he thinks." His smugness was wiped away by bitterness. I was on the edge of biting my tongue again and again. Marius glared at me with the understanding I was the one who alerted these men he would be going against their wishes.

Vergard spoke to Marius in the language I could not distinguish earlier. The harsh tones and wincing Marius responded with were unnerving. It's difficult to see Marius in the light as weak. Every few minutes, the man who brought him back downstairs would stick an elbow into his ribs to remind him of his penalty.

Once Vergard finished his tongue lashing with Marius, he directed Jaali to show me to my room so they could deal with Marius privately. A shiver ran down my skin, as if the temperature of the room dropped dramatically. He reminded me to get my vial from the table, then I was escorted up to one of the rooms in the hallway that I had noticed when we first came in. He stopped in the middle of the living room, pointing out the bedroom on the farthest left of the three doors.

"That is your room." He waited for me to walk ahead of him. It seemed unlikely they would simply trust me to stay here while they were downstairs leaving me unattended. I wondered if he was going to lock me in. Then I remembered young Marius was in one of the other two rooms, also unattended. However, he chose to be here. There would be no reason to keep him against his will. It didn't look like the door knob had a lock on it. I must have proved myself trustworthy enough. I paused at the door.

"Go in," Jaali said and sat down at the table in the living room. I realized I wasn't as trusted as I thought. He would be my watchdog. "You will wake early to work. Go to sleep."

I lay on the dingy mattress on the floor, staring at the ceiling, replaying what Feng said about my father having spent his last days in this room, lying on this same mattress. Of course, that could have been a lie meant to rattle me. It was hard to believe it was a lie, though. Maybe I wanted it to be true because it made me feel closer to my dad than I had felt since he died. I rolled over to my side and scanned the dark room. My eyes were adjusting enough that I could make out a desk, a nightstand, and a small closet. What if my dad left something here? I've read about how prisoners of war leave behind markings on the wall of their cells. It's possible; he could've left something to show he was here. I couldn't turn on the light because my bodyguard out in the living room would see it spilling underneath the bottom of my bedroom door. I was exhausted anyway, so I made a mental plan for a room inspection the next morning as I drifted off to sleep.

The first ray of sunlight shining through the bare window woke me from my sleep. At first, I was confused as to where I was and what was happening, but it didn't take long for my brain to remind me that I was possibly going to die today. I decided to check on my watchdog, and crept over to the door. I turned the handle slowly so as to not make a sound, and peered through the tiniest crack I could manage. Jaali was still seated at the table, reading something from his phone. He didn't look up at me, but he knew I was there.

"Morning. Do you need to use the restroom?"

I opened the door all the way. No use in acting like I wasn't there. He clearly knew I was. "Yes. Where is it?"

He looked up and pointed to the room next to me. Two bedrooms, one bathroom. That made sense. Logically, I knew where young Marius was staying now. Slowly, I left my room and walked into the bathroom, feeling his eyes follow my steps. I closed the door behind me and exhaled with it. The bathroom was fitting of the entire house. I've used outhouses in better shape. I wasn't sure if the toilet was really going to flush, and I felt my hands would have stayed cleaner if I didn't try to wash them in the grimy sink. The mirror above the sink was cloudy and covered with multi colored scum. I glanced at myself, barely visible in the haze. Another deep breath before I returned to my room.

Back in my room, I searched every square inch. Maybe there would be a syringe around here. I started with the mattress, lifting it off the floor, checking for any ripped seams wherein my dad could have hidden something. I felt the entire surface area of the floorboards for any loose panels, then moved onto the closet, reaching my hand up into the empty shelf and then along the walls. I was beginning to feel foolish, considering if there might even be a surveillance camera somewhere, but I had already committed to this idea and so kept my search alive.

I stood in front of the desk, contemplating the obviousness of the only furniture in the room other than the nightstand. No one would 'hide' something in this desk. Nevertheless, I shrugged my shoulders and continued on with my ridiculous hunt, opening the only drawer which ran across the top of it. Inside was a single ink pen and several loose pieces of paper. Each piece was blank. Disappointed, I closed the drawer and inspected every edge of that desk. I pulled it away from the wall to check behind it, as well. About to give up my investigation, I took the drawer out of the desk in case something may have fallen behind it. On my hands and knees, I peered into the space that held the drawer. My eyes fell upon a folded piece of paper hanging on a screw. I ripped it off and unfolded it in slow motion. I recognized the handwriting right away.

How many times had my dad and I sketched out plans to build something and recorded our findings as we tested theories? It's almost as if he left this here for me to find it. He knew I would come. It became difficult to read the paper through the blur in my eyes. I put the page down, wiped my hands across my face, and deeply inhaled to clear my mind. My dad had left me the names of every single founding member of The Reckoning, along with each of their roles in the organization and locations. I was right about Vergard. He was the man in charge. My bodyguard, Jaali, was an assassin.

Reading the details rebirthed fear into my body. I became nervous about holding this paper so freely in the open when these men could appear in my room at any moment without warning. I folded it back up and as I did, I caught Feng's name. He was the organization's number two after Vergard, and their top assassin. I recalled the naive moment I felt he was the safest of these men simply because he wore a wedding band. This was the man who took personal responsibility for the torture and murder of my dad. With the note hidden inside my bra, I decided to make the first move. I exited the room and prepared for my first day of work for The Reckoning.

"When can I get started today?" Jaali looked up from his phone again. This time he seemed annoyed that I was distracting him, which made me feel uneasy knowing what he did for a living. He was difficult to read. He hadn't given me much to go on the evening before either. Jaali didn't seem like a man who liked many people. I didn't want to give him any reason to have a particular dislike for me.

"Let's go ask Marius, yes?" I winced at the thought of seeing Marius today after hanging him out to dry with his superiors last night. He rose from his seat and led me back to the basement. Neither Vergard or Feng were there. It was still early, so it didn't surprise me. It's not like they would be staying in this dump overnight. I looked around the room and noticed a large man hunched in the dark corner on the other side of the basement.

"Marius, get up. Dr. Barrett is ready to start the day. Get her to the hospital." He lifted his head from resting on his arms and let his legs fall flat to the floor. I could tell he was looking in my direction but I couldn't see his face in the darkness of the room. As he made his way off the ground and into a stand, he groaned with discomfort. I didn't really understand why he would've slept here in the corner of the basement. Why didn't he leave, too? Mid thought, he stepped into the light and I felt my hand move toward my mouth in shock.

Consciously, I moved it back to my side and blinked until my mouth closed. It was clear that he had been badly beaten last night. I felt responsible for that. Still catching myself feeling sympathy for this man, I had to remind myself why I was here in the first place. I wanted to put those bruises on him myself many times over the previous day. He did this to himself. I could see though, he was having a difficult time viewing it that way. From the look in his eyes, he clearly blamed me for his long night. He grabbed my arm hard and pulled me up the stairs.

"Ow, Marius! Stop it!" I swatted at his grasp on my arm, trying to get him to loosen his hold. In turn, he gripped tighter. I supposed he felt I deserved a bruise of my own.

He drove us to the same hospital he had me hostage at earlier. This made sense. I was pulled along in the same hold all the way to a room far back in a wing of the hospital. It was a rather decent laboratory that at first glance looked well supplied with all I would need. No doubt Marius was the organizer of this working environment, under the impression it would be his. I was sure that having me here to take it from him wasn't a highlight of his day either. Having addressed my pity for him and leaving it behind in the basement, I turned to him and took the opportunity to put a bit of salt into his wounds.

"Thank you for getting this ready for me Marius. It looks as though I'll have everything I need. Will you be staying to assist me?" His gulp was easily recognized. I pulled the vial from my pocket and walked away from him to get started.

"Don't bother looking for a syringe to empty your vial into. When I got everything ready for you, I made sure to remove all of the syringes so you could focus on your task. Let me know if you need my assistance any further."

Every chance I could, I requested his assistance—and with each request, I could physically feel his hatred grow. It was becoming a tool of mental strength for me. It didn't take very long before I had everything initially set up. I was ready to begin the separation of the serum when Vergard appeared.

The power he held was apparent with how he glided into the lab, resembling a snake. Taking in the markings left on Marius, he smirked with a pleased response to his artwork. I couldn't picture Vergard did the damage to Marius, though. He seemed too graceful to physically beat someone. I could, however, picture Feng enjoying a little bit of aggression. Vergard seemed like he would enjoy watching it, though.

"Good morning, Marius. You look well today. Have you eaten yet? No? Why don't you head down to the cafeteria and grab a bite to eat. Bring back something for Dr. Barrett, as well. I'm sure she's hungry." I acknowledged his offer and smiled politely at Vergard before returning to my task. Marius looked over his shoulder at the two of us alone on his way out the door. He almost looked concerned.

Vergard pulled a chair from across the room, screeching it along the floor until he was about a foot from me and then sat down. He slinked back and watched me through his icy blue eyes. I cannot recall ever having felt so creeped out in my entire life. He didn't say a single word. Just watched me and pursed his lips together like I was performing for him. When I could stand it no longer, I stopped my work and turned toward him, making sure to stare dead in his eyes.

"Do you have any questions? I would be happy to answer them for you." I wanted this man to understand that I would be no damsel in distress for him.

He met my challenge and rose to his feet. He took his lanky fingers and grazed them across my cheek before wrapping them through my hair and slowly tightening them into a fist. It didn't hurt, but it was clear he was sending me a message. Still, I did not break my gaze.

"Such a woman, wanting to explain things to me." He dropped his hand from my hair and returned to his chair. "No need, Dr. Barrett. I'm happy to watch."

Marius took his time leaving me alone with this detestable man before he came bursting back through the door with a bagel and black coffee for me. What a relief it was to have my lesser evil return. He dropped the bagel on the counter space next to where I was working and slammed the coffee down, spilling some on the countertop. I pretended not to notice his tantrum and picked up the coffee to take a gulp.

"Thank you Marius. This is exactly what I needed."

Vergard rose again from his chair and swiftly walked toward the door. Over his shoulder he commanded Marius to stay with me until I was done for the day.

"What happened while I was gone, Tay? Did you have any other intel on me you decided to report to my boss? Can I expect another beating this evening?"

"We didn't speak to each other. I worked. He watched. He's a creepy guy."

"Creepy? You have no idea what that man is capable of. Creepy doesn't begin to cover it."

We worked in silence for the next few hours. It felt familiar. I could've let myself fall into a natural rhythm with Marius again. I had to remind myself that he was a monster, like Vergard. The problem was that Marius believed he was the good guy. He thought the fight that The Reckoning brought was a just one.

"Be ready to go in a half hour. I'm getting tired and hungry. Plus, we have to stop for food to bring back to my kid version. You're going to get to meet him when you deliver his food. I'm not even allowed to see him now, thanks to you."

A soft tap on his bedroom door and I waited in anticipation to meet the young version of my life's nemesis. My hands wrapped around the bag of food I was to deliver to the boy before returning to my room for the evening as directed. Marius had already gone downstairs to meet with Vergard. I wasn't sure who else was down there but I could hear some commotion and laughter that wasn't audible yesterday. It was still earlier than I had arrived the previous day, so it could've been the difference in time. I couldn't fathom why there were so many planning meetings going on now. Their big assault wouldn't happen for over a decade. I supposed the meticulous planning and plotting can be credited for their successful attack in the future. The boy opened his door and flooded my heart. There stood a sweet, wide-eyed boy. Sadness was fresh on his face. I had to fight every urge in my being from saving him. If I ever needed proof of the goodness that lived in that man, it was right here in this boy's face.

"Hi there. My name is Taden. I work with your friends and they asked me to bring you dinner. Are you hungry?" He nodded and reached for the bag. "It looks like you could use some company. Why don't you come out into the living room and eat? I still have my dinner to eat as well. We can eat together. Wouldn't that be so much better than sitting alone in our rooms, shoving food in our faces?" Spread across his face was the start of the famously charming Marius smile. Out of the corner of my eye, I spotted Marius's duffle bag—the one he brought in with us last night, containing the other timed-release band. I busied setting the food onto the table in the living room and sent young Marius to locate some forks in the kitchen. Faster than I had ever moved before, I lifted the bag from his room and dropped it into mine. We reconvened back in the living room at the same time. He was suspect of nothing. One advantage of his youth was his lack of suspicion.

I hadn't considered that Marius was new to speaking English as a teenager, but it was clear that the teenage version of him was having a hard time following our conversation. I slowed my speaking pace and let the boy do more of the talking. Not wanting to miss an opportunity to affect his future into a more positive outcome, I felt compelled to plant the seeds of good intentions into his impressionable mind. Carefully selecting the most impactful words I could, my mission had launched. I was consumed with advising the boy to be cautious of his friends downstairs, that they weren't good people and that as soon as he could, he should get far from them. Unfortunately, I was so wrapped up in my vision to save Marius from himself, I didn't hear his adult counterpart return to the living room behind me. Not sure how long he stood there, or how much he heard, but when the boy looked from my soapbox to someone behind me my gut felt the danger I had stepped into.

Adult Marius's brace on my arm told me that he was definitely more angry with me now than at any other point so far. I had made my move to redirect his younger self. He dragged me toward my bedroom and I winced at the pain shooting through my arm. It was possible he might snap a bone. At the opening of the door he peered over his shoulder to confirm no one was around. The boy had been sent back to his room before Marius unleaded his wrath upon me. Sure of his clearance, he threw me into the room and shut the door behind him. Stumbling backward, I caught myself just before falling to the floor. I could hear Abel's words in my head, coaching me never to lose my footing.

"It's always harder to win a fight if you're on the floor, Taden," he preached at me.

The anger Marius held for me was palpable. I sensed his intentions were to end it here and now. I wouldn't let this put me into a panic though. Analytically, I placed my feet apart to find my center of gravity in case he tried to displace me again. My brain stayed busy retrieving self-defense moves. It wasn't logical for him to kill me yet. He needed me for his role in The Reckoning. He probably just wanted to hurt me, now that he had free reign to do it.

I understood his hatred for me, I hated him in return and would end it for him if I had the chance, even if it meant I would be stuck here. Marius had taken so much from me that I could never get back—but then I thought maybe I could. It didn't look good, though, and I was cornered with no way out. There was no one to rescue me. If I was going to live, I would have to stand my ground and fight to the death.

I found myself feeling pity for him. Even with murder in his eyes.

Marius was void of love. It didn't matter how much I loved him, he wasn't capable of it. Maybe *that's* why he hated me so much. He knew he could never feel the love in his life that I felt. He had lost his ability to be human with the rage that took over in his heart after his sister's murder. It couldn't be more obvious to me after meeting the version of himself that hadn't hardened yet.

Maybe time travel could resolve The Reckoning by simply saving Marius's sister. To think his sister's death might have been the kindling of this war was mind-altering.

He was breathing at me like a matador coming in for his bull—nostrils flared and eyes went blank. This was particularly concerning, because it meant he wasn't clearly thinking about how he needed me as a pawn.

I had to bring him out of his rage. "Marius, what are you doing? You know you need me to do work for you." He kept inching forward. I backed away. In the most quiet and clear manner I could muster, I proceeded, "Can you hear me? I know you are angry about me talking to your younger self. If you want to get back to your sister, you need time travel uncoded. You need the serum. Otherwise, this will all be in vain." As if a battery was pulled from his control panel, he stopped.

He turned from me and ran his hands across his face and through his hair, like he was trying to wipe away his primal desire to take my life.

Without hesitation, I took the opportunity to dive at the duffle bag. The timed-release band would be my only attempt at escaping. Frantically, I unzipped the bag, allowing my fingers to fumble around for the band. The feeling of momentous glory at finally having it in my grasp was quickly revoked by Marius's hands around my neck.

There wasn't a way to physically beat this mammoth. I wanted him to know I understood his pain, even if he took my life. I gasped, "Marius, I'm sorry they killed her. I'm sor…" He choked the last words out of my throat. I could hear Abel screaming in the distance. He was fighting Marius off me—

But I was tired of all of this fighting. I went in the other direction, toward my parents.

CHAPTER 16

ABEL

My mission was always to protect Taden. Before it was even officially my mission.

We had several classes together in college, prior to her awareness I existed. Since the first day of the first class we shared, I didn't mind her ignorance of me as long as I could be around her. Truly fitting her personality, she arrived well before anyone else. Her seat was front and center. Her notebook was already open, highlighter and ink pens ready to work, and her nose in a book. She didn't look up for a single soul until the professor announced the start of the class. I sat a couple rows over so I could get a good look at her without seeming like a stalker. My amusement grew as the class progressed and there was not a question asked for which her hand didn't shoot up to answer. Typically, the classic kiss-up routine was obnoxious, but that wasn't what Taden was about. I could genuinely tell she was on fire for this stuff.

Her main concern was acquiring information. The more of it a person had to offer, the more she would gravitate to that person. You could pour knowledge into her and she would drink it up as if it contained life. I didn't feel a bruised ego that Taden didn't know I shared the Earth with her, because she didn't know anyone did unless it led to her learning.

A few semesters later, I finally got my moment when luck paid me a visit and we were paired up in a group project. It was my chance to make an impression on her, and I would not take it for granted. Careful not to blow it, I actually studied harder in preparation to work with Taden than I did for any of my classes—and I worked hard in all of my classes. The payoff came the moment she actually saw me for the first time. It felt like jumping from a plane in those terrifying yet exhilarating seconds before the parachute opens.

After that first assigned group project, we worked together regularly. We worked together not only in assigned groups, but often by choice in the library. I'm not sure how anyone could understand the way I felt to have Taden Barrett choose me as someone she wanted to spend time with outside of class. I could care less that all we ever did was study. It was enough for me. I never made a move to be more with her. She was not someone you rushed into anything or distracted from her goals. Time was the only way I would show her my heart.

There was one stand-out day when I thought Taden might have picked up on my feelings for her. We were both in the library, working on a major report independently. I looked up from my research to find Taden staring at me from across the room. She had an incredible look of longing on her face, which I was powerless to overcome. It took my breath away and locked me in. I realized seconds into my illusion she was simply daydreaming in my direction. While it was disappointing, her beautiful face canceled out my chagrin.

She became embarrassed when she realized she was staring and immediately turned bright red. It was probably one of the most endearing features of hers. But then...then she looked back and smiled an incredibly gorgeous smile at me. I couldn't resist.

CHAPTER 17

Bursting open the door, I found her—but too late. My arrival timed up to Marius squeezing one last breath out of Taden. At this point, having known Taden since I was eighteen, I've spent over thirteen years of my life watching over her and making certain she is safe and happy just to watch her die at his hands. It was beyond my ability to digest. I refused to accept this as our outcome. With a ferocity I never knew lived within me, I attacked her murderer. I didn't even use my gun. I wanted to feel my hands bring each blow to his body and finally wrap around his neck the way he hurt her. I was disappointed by how quickly he succumbed.

A numbness settled into my bones, preparing me for the loss of Taden. I fell to her side, checking for a pulse and desperately listening for any evidence of breathing. I was too late. Consumed with agony and disbelief, I pulled her across my legs and cradled her in my arms. Taden's lifeless body dangled back to the ground.

"Come back. You belong here. Please come back. He's gone. It's over. Please, Taden, you have so much to do. So much left. I love you. Please come back."

I slid her fully onto my lap and held her in my arms, rocking back and forth with my face next to hers. Hysterics were taking hold of me when I put my trembling lips onto hers. She was still warm. She had to come back. It wasn't too late. I could still save her. This was my purpose in life, and it had never been so clear. Laying next to her on the floor was a timed-release band.

I strapped the band onto her arm, triggered the alarm that would notify Dakotah she had returned and where to find her, and sent her to the present.

CHAPTER 18

RUTH

We waited anxiously for what felt like an eternity before Abel finally returned. When he did, his face was swollen from crying and he did not have Taden with him.

I felt nauseous. I knew what it meant. I couldn't move or feel or think. My face twisted in confusion as disbelief and anger took hold of me.

I ran at Abel with my fists up, beating his chest on impact. "No! No! You were supposed to save her."

He didn't defend himself, taking each hit as they came. He cried. Unashamed, he cried. Abel couldn't offer me words or comfort. He could only cry.

There were no other feelings in my emotional range beyond anger. I was angry she wasn't here with me. She had abandoned me. I was angry Abel was crying and I wasn't. I desperately needed to. The rage bursting from me was enough to take down The Reckoning single handed. It was more than I could handle.

Abel finally caught enough of a breath to deliver his next move. "We have to go. We have to leave right now. There's no more time to waste. She might live. I have to get back to her."

"Wait! She's still alive? Abel, is she okay or not?"

"I don't know for sure. I couldn't feel a pulse but she was warm. I sent her back home. We have to go."

Dr. Pasterski sat in perfect silence on a wingback chair in her book-lined living room, grasping her gun. At the urging of Abel's departure, she went to her desk and pulled out a small, red and gold notebook, onto which she fiercely wrote.

I interrupted her mania. "Dr. Pasterski, we have to leave." She held up her finger at us to wait a minute. The fury with which she penned onto the paper was what my thoughts were doing to my brain. The rhythm pulled me into a facade of calm as I stared at her hand ravaging that paper.

Abel was fumbling around, preparing my timed-release band between bursts of breathing spasms. Everything was in place. We were just waiting on Dr. Pasterski to finish her notes so we could time jump back home.

Thrusting the red and gold book at me, she commanded, "Be sure you give this to your sister's team *as soon as you return,* Ruth. This will save her." At that instruction, Abel finished the reset on the band and sent us back.

When we arrived it had already felt like the longest night of my life, and we still had to get to the site where Taden returned from her time jump. Abel sent Taden back from the site of The Reckoners where he found her. But then he had to come get me from Dr. Pasterski's house which is where we time traveled from. As soon as we regained our equilibrium, we rushed to get to where she was located hoping we would find her alive.

Dakotah and Dr. Pasterski had already tracked the location of her return to the empty lot that in the past, held the house of *The Reckoning*. They got there before us to find her lifeless body in an overgrown field. Abel told us it was the exact location of the room in which Marius killed her. Dakotah feverishly worked at reviving Taden, not knowing if she was truly dead or hanging on by a thread. If it was possible that she hadn't died, Dakotah was doing everything she could to help her hold on for dear life. I stumbled upon the scene and froze at the sight of Taden on the ground. Momentarily, I forgot the salvation from Dr. Pasterski in my hand.

Across from me, Abel watched the revival attempts full of pain and torment, obvious to anyone who had the gall to watch him. He held his face in his hands, trying to reconcile this outcome before he stopped Dakotah. Through more heavy sobs, he managed to say, "Stop. She's gone. Leave her."

I snapped out of my trance and rushed to Dr. Pasterski, who was shining her flashlight at me. "Wait! Dr. Pasterski gave me these notes." I frantically waved it in their faces like I held the elixir of life to save my sister. "She told me I had to get this to you right away, that it would save Taden."

I anxiously glanced between Dakotah reading the notes I had just shoved at her under the thin light Dr. Pasterski held in her hands and my sister's life-less body. Every second that passed felt like an eternity of loss.

I caught the two women exchange a hopeful glance over the information Dr. Pasterski gave us from the past. What happened next pressed the pause button on our grief.

"This could actually work. We might have a chance here," Dakotah exclaimed.

I couldn't passively wait to be let in on the deep magic at work. "Is she going to be okay?"

"Taden talked with me about this possibility the night we agreed to cypher the data."

Dr. Pasterski chimed in, "And Taden and I talked about this several times over the years—but more seriously, the past few months since Taden had finally been able to send animals back."

Dakotah continued, "We have been able to send people only as far back as their age and then return to the future that same distance of time they traveled. Do you follow?"

I nodded impatiently and noticed that Abel had gone to cradle Taden in his arms during the conversation. Since it seemed I understood so far, the explanation resumed.

"If we travel back to before our Taden died while in the past, we should be able to avoid that time loop and jump her back to now before she dies. We can only do this because she died outside of her current time loop."

I couldn't believe what they were saying. My sister was lying dead in Abel's arms, yet if I understood them correctly, they were telling me because she died while time traveling, we could go back and pull her out of her time travel before she got killed, and then this whole experience will have never happened. My head was spinning, but who was I to doubt this crazy science my sister discovered?

Bent down to Abel, Dakotah put her hands on his shoulders. It was clear watching they had created a very close bond. It made sense that they would, while working so closely together on incredible discoveries for years and not being able to discuss any of it with anyone but each other. I've noticed that

they all had an ability to communicate with each other without words. It borderline enraged me that none of them figured out Marius was dirty. I know
they all felt it in their gut. Even Taden.

After a respectful silence for him to make peace with Taden's death, Dakotah spoke to Abel. "You need to go back. We will send you to the spot
ahead of her dying. You get her out of there and bring her home. Do you
hear me?"

Abel was distracted from his grief long enough to consider this plan, but
then he pointed out one major flaw. "Taden has been dead now for more than
a half hour. This is a window of time that will be unaccounted for in her molecular make up. If I go back to before she died and pull her out of the past,
she can only come back to that same distance of time to the present. She will
be missing the time frame starting at her death until I pull her out of the past.
She won't be able to get back to the here and now." He was becoming frantic
as he pointed this out.

Dr. Pasterski nodded in agreement and approval at Abel's postulations.
I couldn't seem to really grasp what he had just said, and it hurt my brain to
try. She then put her finger up and interjected Abel's panic.

"But! Taden also had theorized that if one could be injected with more
molecular energy, then we would be able to override the inability to travel
past your lifetime either forward or backward. She had a notion that the injection had to be a DNA match." And then she turned toward me and raised
her eyebrow.

"I don't have any idea what you are saying, but if you need some part of
me to get my sister back, it's yours. Take it." I ran to Dr. Pasterski, my arms
outstretched for her to stick a needle into them or whatever they needed and
save Taden already.

"My dear," she said to me as she gently put my arms back at my side.
"I know you would sacrifice anything to save your sister." She turned to
Dakotah and Abel, "but could we not spare Ruth the uncomfortable DNA
sample and take the tissue from Taden herself?" They both stared in thought
at her questioning until Dakotah broke the silent concentration with her
conclusion.

"I think it's possible. It could work with Taden's own tissues, or her body
might not recognize them as additional molecular energy since they clone her
own. I mean it is her exact DNA. I don't think now is the time to gamble.
We know that Ruth is a DNA match and that her molecular make up will

match Taden's. If this is going to work at all, we have a more certain chance if we use Ruth's DNA."

As if she were made of glass, Abel, carefully laid Taden back on the ground. He released her only so he could get her back. The three scientists firmed up the plan to travel back and use my DNA to save Taden. The science lingo they spoke with, while foreign to me, translated through their body language and conveyed that there truly was hope she would be alright. It was crazy confusing to feel hope in the face of her death. I needed to be with her, so, I took my turn saying goodbye.

Hope is not what pulled me down onto my knees though. My proximity to her death dissolved the anticipation that began to filter from her friends. There on the icy, wet grass, I scooped her into my arms and rested my head on her chest, wishing I could hear a beating rhythm. What I coveted was denied by stillness. It was enough to burn my heart to emptiness. I didn't even notice I had finally let go of my rage until her clothes were soaked with my tears. The release transformed my ravenous anger into delicate pain. Anger had strength. Although I was becoming broken in the pain, it was so much less demanding of my body than the anger. I noticed a piece of paper sticking out of the top of Taden's shirt near her chest. Unfolding it, I read a list of names, jobs, and locations.

After their plan had been roughly laid out, Abel faithfully returned to Taden. He lifted her from me tenderly. I loved him for the way he held her. I held the list up to him.

"I found this on her. It looks important." He took the paper from me before carrying Taden off toward the lights shining from the car we arrived in. Silently, we followed behind.

The drive back to the lab to prepare for this rescue mission was so fast it felt like time travel. Although it was now the dead of night and everyone was exhausted, her team did not waste any time. Every second added meant another onto the jump she would need to complete with my DNA.

I stood in the middle of my sister's science laboratory, her heaven, and watched her people bustling here and there, busy with the most important task she had ever given them. Dr. Pasterski approached me to introduce the bigwigs Taden worked for.

"Ruth dear, I want you to meet Danika Farkas. She is in charge of the agency that employs your sister. Everyone that has a role in this mission is here to be sure it goes off without a hitch."

I tried very hard to smile politely but I'm pretty sure my post-traumatic stress state came across like I was crazy. "Nice to meet you. Ms. Farkas. Taden has told me nothing about you, like she promised."

Welp, I blew that introduction.

Dakotah anxiously interrupted, ready for my DNA. Relieved about my early dismissal, I politely apologized and excused myself.

The DNA they required from me wasn't as simple as a blood withdrawal like I thought it was going to be. They actually needed to take a sample of my tissue. I didn't really care. I couldn't feel pain, and I couldn't feel fear. I paused somewhere in the middle of ultimate loss. All I wanted was to get my sister back. It felt like I was watching my life through a screen. I could see Dakotah place a scalpel onto my skin and slice it open. There was nothing to feel.

She looked up at me with concern. "Are you doing okay, Ruth?" I barely nodded but it was enough for her to continue. After I was bandaged up, I accepted the scalding hot cup of coffee she offered me then returned to my front-row viewing of the lab.

Abel was briefing his tactical team of the locations and names of The Reckoners to take down. I listened. I shouldn't have. In hindsight, I never should have heard the details of my sister's murder. Having a visual picture of that horrendous man with his hands around her neck sparked a hate I had never felt in all my life.

All together, about three hours had passed from Taden's timeline when they were ready with her timed-release band, which now included enough of my DNA to get her back here.

Abel and The Patriot heads had finished preparing the tactical team of soldiers he would be taking back with him and were leaving to go back to the empty lot where we found Taden. This was the location where she would be in the hands of Marius when they time jumped. Abel's team would ascend upon The Reckoners there and kill them all. This was also where she would return with Abel after he rescued her, so I insisted I go, too. I would not sit here and idly wait for her to return like I agreed to do the last time. No one argued with me on the matter. I think they were all either slightly afraid of me or for me. Either way, they weren't willing to challenge my emotional state.

Taden's body rested on a lonely metal table in the back of the room. I trod over to her, kissed her forehead, and whispered, "See you soon."

Taking one last look at her I wondered if her body would still be here once we fixed her timeline, or if this body of hers would dissolve into thin air.

THE RECKONING

Everyone piling out of the building was so loaded up with gear you would have presumed a war had begun. That's when I remembered that was precisely what had happened. This rescue attempt wasn't only going to save my sister from her untimely death; it would also terminate The Reckoning so this war will have never started in the first place. I again wondered how many other small changes would be made to our timelines. Maria popped into my mind repeatedly.

Oh God! Maria! If anything had happened to her during this terrorist attack, she had to be restored, too. Then, I thought about the possibility that our paths might not cross with the change that was about to happen in the timeline. I couldn't linger on this idea. Pushing it out of my mind, I ran after the soldiers flooding out of the building.

Back at the site, I stared blankly at the empty lot. It was difficult to process that this land once held a home that safeguarded the people who would try to take over our country and ultimately murder my father and my sister. As I stood here on this soil, in another timeline people were working on that plan. I turned my watch onto Abel and his soldiers preparing to stop all of it.

I believed he would come back with her alive this time.

CHAPTER 19

ABEL

No one at that house was to be left alive except Taden. I was dead set to kill Marius again. One bullet, this time. No time for my rage and revenge. Just save Taden.

Our jump back to the past was intense. It was the first jump with a large group. All six of my team members arrived safely. We set up a perimeter outside the house and moved directly into our positions. I don't remember taking another breath until the moment Marius released his hands from Taden's neck.

He was distracted by the surprise of my entrance. I was only minutes earlier than I was the first time this scenario played out. Those extra minutes were all the time needed for the rest of my life. Taden saw her moment and reached into Marius's pants to pull out a knife, that in the next breath she pushed into his chest. He turned back to her, his face contorted with confusion, then dropped to the floor, laboriously breathing and holding his wound. The blood on his hands informed him of his defeat.

As he died, Taden, who had every right to feel nothing but hate for this man, told him how she was sorry he lost his sister and that she would do what she could to honor his sister's life and wrongful death. Instead of allowing that horrific man to die alone, she offered him kindness. Taden's generous hand rested on his selfish one. It should have been hard for me to watch, but I could not see anything but amazing goodness and beauty in her. Before long, he exhaled one last time and was, at last, gone.

There she was. Living. Breathing. I dropped my gun to the ground, for she had saved herself. Diving to her, my longing hands instinctively found their way to her face and cradled each side. I could feel the vitality of her skin under my thumbs, which caressed her glowing cheeks.

In response, she placed her hands onto mine, granting me the sweetness I had craved since the moment I first laid eyes on her. Then and there, she looked straight into my soul and I could no longer hide it from her. She could see herself in my reflection. The unveiling of my core didn't make her flinch, or blink, or turn bright red. My brain sent pleasure synapses shooting throughout my entire body. "Taden, I..." and before I could finish my words, she nodded her head allowing her beautiful mouth to curve upward into a genuine smile, revealing her love for me in return.

I pulled her toward me and placed my lips on hers. The heat from her kiss melted into mine. I wanted nothing more from this life.

It was then that I remembered we had to leave.

She didn't question me or hesitate as I strapped her timed-release band onto her arm. I held her hand with no intention of ever letting go again, and together we jumped through time.

CHAPTER 20

RUTH

We discovered that, should our timeline change as a result of actions taken during a time travel, if we were a part of the time travel, we did not lose any memory of our previous timeline.

I remember Taden returned from a time travel dead. I remember the agony of losing her. My memories are clear and vivid to the point of Abel leaving to return to the past again to get Taden. I stayed back and waited for him to bring her home alive. The next memory gets a bit fuzzy, like watching a poorly-edited movie. All of a sudden, he was in front of us, with her, totally fine. He went to the minute before Marius killed her, got her, and returned. Essentially, whatever I was doing during his rescue mission, I have lost. I can assume I was wrecked with worry that Taden was dead and my actions were consumed with that event, but since she didn't die, I've lost the previous timeline in my memory.

It seemed like even with the adjustments that our timelines underwent, we were meant to keep the encounters that ultimately brought us to our purpose in life.

We found out that although we didn't lose our previous timeline memories, we *were* able to gain new memories from the changes that occurred. It was hard to detect that a memory was new at first. Like I said, it was akin to watching a badly-edited film.

Through careful reflection and documentation under Taden's science team, they found discrepancies between our old memories and our current ones. For example, as a result in a change to our timeline we might have missed out on a relationship we used to have with a loved one. Some scenarios gifted to us memories of a previously lost person we now had as a part of our lives.

It is strange listening to Taden, Abel, and me talk with Dakotah, Dr. Pasterski, and the Patriot Party about the time jumps, because our separate memories of the events don't always align.

In our new timelines, The Reckoning was, in essence, wiped from the agenda of The Patriot Party. After Taden returned from the rescue mission, The Patriot soldiers, under Abel's direction, launched an assault plan to return back at the exact location Taden was staying to wipe out all of The Reckoners. His orders were to kill everyone in the house and in the hospital. Taden could not condone killing young Marius. She relentlessly fought for his rescue and placement in a safe haven. Abel was discouraged at the thought of saving such an abomination of a human being, but he was not of character to stand in Taden's way of something she so strongly fought for. The Patriot Party, on the other hand, were not supportive of Taden's bleeding heart for Marius. They wanted him removed from the possibility of future attacks. My sister persisted until the day of the launch back. She was on the team to rescue the boy she so deeply needed to save. I was also participating in this time jump. It was unacceptable that I would even be considered to stay behind. I would not allow my sister to return back to her death scene, to save the young version of her killer, in a house full of the men who hired him to murder her.

The Patriots knew ahead of time that these memories would be erased for them, and the plan of how the time travelers would inform them of the lost details had already been put into place. The soldiers were to be integral in proving the data we were piecing together for everyone. Without them, we might have looked like raving lunatics to the Patriots. Having six soldiers verify the concept of the The Reckoning and the mission to stop them from terror activity made all of it a lot less impossible to explain.

The Patriot Party was still an essential organization, because our government's weaknesses and political corruption remained and still needed to be addressed. My dad's list of all The Reckoners that Taden found in the past helped keep track of any people that might become loose ends.

Taden convinced Danika to launch a team to go back in time to save Marius's sister the day she came to our country for asylum. She persuaded the Patriots that it was the most effective measure they could take to ensure that Marius would not turn toward any terrorist role, against our government, who might attract him had his sister died the same way. She made sure that his sister was granted citizenship and provided for in a foster refugee program.

Taden finally made the time jump to visit our dad. Dr. Pasterski had told Taden it was this visit that set in motion her time travel mission. She went to him, told him what she knew she had to in order to keep her life on track, but then she made a huge change. Taden told him he was going to be killed by Feng and how to avoid it.

I am grateful I didn't forget Maria. The impression she left in my life could never be undone. I will forever carry heartache that our altered timelines didn't allow us to cross paths but I'd take the heartache over ever forgetting her.

My new timeline developed who I became and what I needed in life differently than my original. I have memories of who I used to be before I met Maria and who I became because of knowing her but in this new timeline, I didn't become 'The Ruth' that knew Maria. So I guess that's why our paths didn't cross.

Of course, I tried to find her. Why wouldn't I? She didn't exist. It was like she vanished from thin air. I checked into everything I knew about her; where she said she grew up, went to school, where her family lived. Nothing turned up. Taden suggested I ask Dr. Pasterski to help me find her because she could pull some government strings.

What amounted from her intel was that Maria was originally tied to the organization of The Reckoning but because their plots were never initiated after Abel and his men took out the founders, Maria didn't come to our country in the first place. I suppose I could've tracked her down but it didn't seem like that's how it should happen. We were not the same people that we were in L.A.

The complicated part, well, who am I kidding? This whole damn thing was complicated. But, one of the tricky things was that tangled up with my heart ache for Maria was also a joy I didn't have before.

I now had amazing memories of my dad that weren't there previously. Like him taking me and Taden to a Daddy Daughter Dance, or helping us with our homework, and dropping us off at the mall to hang out with our friends. All of these memories that I can *remember needing* so bad in my life without him.

The most life changing of my new memories were the ones that I had gained of how tenderly he cared for our mother as she slowly and painfully died of cancer. That alone, was enough change in my timeline to completely alter the Ruth I was into the Ruth I am now.

After I graduated from our community college, I moved to New York to stay somewhat near my dad and Taden and worked at the partnering public relation's firm I worked for in L.A. in my other timeline.

My dad ended up moving in with Dr. Pasterski not too long after Taden and I were both out of the house. Maybe it should be weird that they sort of fell together but it really wasn't. I know my dad loved my mom more than anything on this planet. My mom knew that too. I guess part of me thinks that Dr. Pasterski and my dad needed companionship. Loneliness is painful and not what I want for either of them. So, I'm happy they have each other.

At least a year passed before I had the courage to find Trey and Jade. I knew they wouldn't know me. Our timelines had been altered with the absence of the *The Reckoning* so that our meeting together didn't need to happen.

First, I found Jade. She was actually pretty easy to locate on social media. I perused through several delightful pictures of her with her husband and son. Her son looked just like her. Comically, she was at a New York Jets football game in one of them. Contrary to her self proclaimed hatred of the sport, it looked like she was enjoying herself. I couldn't help but chuckle to myself about that.

Oddly enough, she had been involved in the very same foster refugee program that Taden placed Marius's sister in. Jade spent decades as an advocate for young refugees fostering several youth until they were of age to become independent or connected with family members who could care for them. I like to think that this was no coincidence. Also, I choose to believe that Jade was connected to one of my timelines for this reason.

Finally, I traveled to the motel that safeguarded me the day The Reckoning began, where I met Trey. I needed to see Trey in person. It wasn't enough just to find his presence online. Walking up to the door, greeted by the neon sign, I noticed I was sweating through my nerves. It was tense not knowing what I would find or if he would even be there.

He *was* there. Same sweet attention to my entrance.

"Good Afternoon Miss, how can I help you?"

"I would like to book a room for this weekend. Do you have any vacancies? I was hoping you had room 3 available?"

I requested the room I stayed in last time I was here unable to stop the toothy grin taking hold of me. If I didn't tone it down, he was going to think I was flirting with him.

"Sure, do. I'll get that taken care of right away."

I noticed his photograph in a plaque on the wall behind him with the caption 'Manager' underneath it. Beaming with pride for my lost little brother, I couldn't stop myself from gushing.

"Wow! I have the manager taking care of me. Well done. I mean, congratulations on such an important position and at your age. You must be quite impressive."

Yep, I could see from his uncomfortable smile in return, he definitely thought I was super weird. Trey finished my booking arrangements and sent me to my room rather quickly after that.

I wish I could've chatted with him more but I honestly didn't want to creep him out any further and really it was exactly what I had hoped for. The motel booking was just an excuse to see Trey, I didn't intend to stay for the weekend but I for sure wanted to go to my room and breath the musty air for some time. After all, it was here that I lost so much but also gained in return.

We learned that every single time jump has major effects on how we live our current lives. Messing with the past can create new branches of events in our timeline, making it an insurmountable challenge to find the way back down the stream of time along the correct path to the now. I hope Taden's science never gets into the wrong hands. It was too close to happening with The Reckoning, and the thought of it gives me nightmares.

CHAPTER 21

TADEN

Reflecting on the morning when we became disconnected, I remember vividly where I was, what I was doing, and each thought that unraveled as I learned of the truth.

I realize now that in order to come together, we first had to fall apart.

It was in the ashes that I was able to sift through for the true love that I deserved, the passion that drove me to joy, and the courage to find myself.

It is to be in the anarchy of revolution where a peaceful system can finally be birthed.

When we as a country, maybe for the first time in history, can live the foundational beliefs that all of us deserve a voice and to be validated, peace is possible.

Traveling back into my past allowed me to see that I never have to say goodbye to my mom.

She would *always* be with me.

In all of my timelines.

CONTACT THE AUTHOR

Follow D.M. Taylor on social media
Facebook – D.M. Taylor
Instagram – @dmtaylor925

Sign Up for D.M. Taylor's mailing list
to receive updates on upcoming books in The Reckoning Series.
https://www.subscribepage.com/dmtaylorthereckoning

A NOTE FROM DR. PASTERSKI

Dear Reader,

Please support my girls, Taden and Ruth Barrett, by zipping on over to Amazon and leaving a positive review for D.M. Taylor who told their story of The Reckoning. We really appreciate Ms. Taylor for her dedication to share their story with such care. She is currently collecting the details for the next book, in the series, of my Barrett girls. The best way we can encourage Ms. Taylor to continue is to leave a positive review for The Reckoning on Amazon.

Much love,
Dr. Pasterski

Made in the USA
Coppell, TX
20 February 2020

16038951R00088